Praise for Philip Cioffari's work

JESUSVILLE

"a truly fascinating and worthwhile book" —*NJ Star-Ledger*

"The real star here is the haunted, haunting theme park full of crumbling temples, decrepit mangers and mazes of limbless, decapitated saints and Christs—a metaphor for the religious wasteland of the twenty-first century and a complex character in its own right." —*Booklist*

"Cioffari brings the Bronx to the Wild West, resulting in a tale of sex, drugs and fervor. A work with a strong sense of urgency, Jesusville grapples with the hard issues of faith and doubt, weaves an intricate story of suspense, and builds to an unforgettable finale, builds even, perhaps, to the redemption the novel's characters so fervently seek."
                                    —Alabama Writers Forum

"A profound and thought-provoking read." —*Midwest Book Review*

"page-turning action scenes. . ."   —*Italian Americana*

A HISTORY OF THINGS LOST OR BROKEN

". . .his writing is exquisitely clear and precise. The uncanny, the off-beat, and the incongruous resonate throughout these stories."
                                    —*Southern Humanities Review*

"Cioffari's meticulously crafted stories explode like street-racing muscle cars burning rubber in search of dangerous fun, holy nostalgia, impossible love, and the exchange of dreams across the back roads of America."
                                    —*Paterson Literary Review*

CATHOLIC BOYS

"I recommend it highly." —Bookviews

--"An entertaining story"   —Italian Americana

"Cioffari proves himself not only a powerful writer who has both a sense of character and story, but also a deep thinker. . ." —*Alabama Writers' Forum*

"The story unfolds over the space of a week in short bursts of plot, much like the pacing of television's Law & Order: Special Victims Unit. Aficionados of that program will like this book."
                                    —New Jersey Star-Ledger

DARK ROAD, DEAD END

"A novel that provides considerable insight within a fictional context."
—New Jersey Star-Ledger

"A fine novel about Florida's illegal exotic animal trade."
—*All Things Crime*

"A suspenseful eco-thriller." —*Publisher's Weekly*

"narrative prowess, language with poetic precision . . . a thriller, rife with danger and tension" —*Italian Americana*

THE BRONX KILL

"It's the brooding atmosphere that truly packs a punch. Readers will gladly lose themselves in this novel's sense of foreboding."
—Kirkus Reviews

"Interesting revelations in this tale of loyalty, lost innocence, and redemption." —*Ellery Queen Mystery Magazine*

"A gripping novel." —*New Jersey Star Ledger*

"Unique, impressively crafted, and an inherently riveting read from beginning to end." —*Midwest Book Review*

"A taut, tense, and atmospheric tale. Richly-developed characters and seductive, suspenseful storyline. A truly thought-provoking tale."
—*Mystery Tribune*

"An enjoyable read about secrets, suspense, and loyalty."
—*Futures Mystery Anthology Magazine*

"A mystery wrapped in revenge. A great book." —*Writeknit*

A haunting tale. Good writing. Capable characters. Excellent plot.
—*Bookloons*

"An engrossing page-turner." —*Italian Americana*

"A compelling web of complex situations andcharacters. An excellent and exciting read!" —*Readers' Favorite*

IF ANYONE ASKS,
SAY I DIED FROM THE
HEARTBREAKING BLUES

Philip Cioffari

LIVINGSTON PRESS

The University of West Alabama

Typesetting and page layout: Sarah Coffey, Joe Taylor
Proofreading: Joe Taylor
Cover layout: Sarah Coffey

Portions of this novel previously appeared, in altered form, in

Italian Americana
The Westchester Review

The author wishes to thank the staff of Livingston Press,
Joe Taylor, and Beth "Jaden" Terrell for their help
in preparing this novel.

IF ANYONE ASKS,
SAY I DIED FROM
THE HEARTBREAKING BLUES

For John Hall

PART ONE
TRY THE IMPOSSIBLE

—1—

The Bronx. June 22nd, 1960

Joey Hunter, known in the neighborhood as *Hunt,* turned eighteen the day of his senior prom, the most hopeful day of his young life—or so he believed—because it would be his first date with Debby Ann Murphy.

That morning he waited in his *Religion in Society* class as Brother Aloysius James, blond hair ascending in waves from his soft pink forehead, clapped his hands to call them to attention. Forty boys, paired into reluctant couples, glared at Brother from either end of the St. Helena's Boys' Division basketball court, their faces in the gym's unflattering light a mix of curiosity, amusement, resentment and outrage.

"Why we gotta do this?" from Kevin Flanagan, his face dominated by little red volcanoes.

"Why can't we use real girls?" This time the question came from Hunt's assigned partner, Sal Buccarelli, first string varsity linebacker, known on the gridiron as Sal the Butcher and, in the after-school hours, as leader of a local gang of would-be toughs called the Brandos.

Brother Aloysius turned to face Sal of the massive shoulders. "We want you to be ready for them, that's why. Tonight at the prom we want you all to behave like the gentlemen we know you can be." *And not the hairy apes you so often are*, his muttered aside so soft only Hunt caught it.

Brother flicked the switch on the turntable and set the needle delicately on the vinyl: the trombone sound of *Moonlight Serenade* filled the gym's barren spaces. Never mind that the big band era had passed, that the boys before him were now dancing to Bill Haley and the Comets, *this*—Brother A believed—was music with elegance and grace. He saw it as his duty to bring civilization to their imprisoned, barbarian hearts. "I need a volunteer," he called out sharply.

Instinctively he turned to Hunt.

"Oh no, Brother. I'm always the girl. Sal never lets me be the guy."

With relief, Hunt watched Brother re-direct his attention to Sal. Something about the over-sized, lumbering linebacker and self-proclaimed gang leader—with a face the texture of stucco and eyes the color of an overcast sky—being led around the gym in the feminine role seemed to tickle Brother's fancy. "Sallie," he said, using the nickname Sal detested.

"Nah, Brudda. Not me. Not me."

But Brother Aloysius marched to him, bowed briefly and said in a loud clear voice, "May I have the honor of this dance?" He cupped his hand firmly around Sal's waist. "Hand on her hip," he instructed the class, "not where you'd like it to be, ha-ha. Your touch should be firm but gentle. Take her right hand, extend your arm and lead her, *glide* her, into the music. At the prom tonight, apply the moral standards we've discussed in class. Treat her with respect. Treat her like she was your sister."

A collective groan rose around him.

Brother Aloysius, one eye on the less-than-graceful technique of the boys dancing under the back boards and along the foul lines, confided to Hunt later that waltzing with Sal Buccarelli was like pulling a two-ton truck though a muddy ditch.

2

Hunt could empathize. Being shoved around the dance floor by Sal was like being *rammed* by a two-ton truck. Mid-song, Brother guided Sal back to Hunt, muttering before he turned away because he couldn't help himself, "You big oaf."

Sal directed his response to Hunt, as if *he* were the source of the insult. "I ain't no loaf."

"Oaf," Hunt corrected him. "He called you a big *oaf.*"

And for that clarification, Hunt was rewarded with a bloody nose, compliments of Sal during lunch break, as soon as they were out of sight of Brother Aloysius who had cafeteria duty that day.

—2—

More bad luck soon followed.

Because seniors were dismissed at noon on Prom day, Hunt decided to work a few hours at the beach. No sooner had he stepped inside the storeroom when Big Tony barked from his glassed-in office: "Hunter, get in uniform. You're on beach patrol today."

"*Me?*"

"O'Brien's not coming in. We need another Rat out there." In the office doorway, his body appeared like a series of concentric circles: small round head, a larger neck, an even larger gut. "Get in uniform," he said. "Move it."

Normally Hunt's job was *inside* the storeroom, supplying soda and ice cream to the roving vendors, the "Desert Rats" who trudged from one end of the beach to the other, lugging a twenty-two pound container of orangeade on their backs or an equally heavy and even more cumbersome metal freezer case of fudgesicles and creamsicles, hawking their wares to the screaming kids and insolent teens who thronged the mile-long crescent beach.

Today there'd be no refuge in the storeroom's air-cooled

interior. Today it would be sweating in the early summer heat, today it would be humiliation after humiliation and the worst of it would be the nightmare of all humiliations, the possibility of being seen by Debby Ann. What kind of respect would she have for a Desert Rat?

After all, he thought in his defense, he deserved to work *in*side. He'd earned it. He worked harder than his co-workers. He could mix a batch of orangeade faster than any of them. *Twice* as fast. He didn't comb his hair over the open vats shedding dandruff flakes the way *they* did. He didn't sneak off every fifteen minutes to crib an ice pop from the freezer.

Nonetheless, Big Tony had spoken, so he donned the requisite monkey suit. With the song, *This is the Night for Love*, trailing him from the storeroom radio, he stepped out onto the boardwalk dressed like a safari guide—round jungle hat, khaki shirt and pants—a silver tank of orangeade strapped to his back.

The fear of running into Debby Ann stopped him dead in his tracks.

In the bright sun of the rotunda he pulled the hat low on his head, then he tried it tilted back. He didn't like it either way. But at least low on his forehead, eyes hidden behind his new Ray-Bans, he was semi-disguised. Or so he hoped.

Across the rotunda, Augie sat on a wall, reading his pocket dictionary. His usual activity—either that or playing his harmonica—though most often his perch was the stoop of his apartment building where he took up residence when his parents weren't around, which seemed to be much of the time.

His full name was Augustus Lionel Robinson: a small kid, quick on his feet, too smart for the ten years he'd spent on this earth. He was the only black kid in their neighborhood, the only black student in St. Helena's grammar school where he was the brightest star of the fifth grade. Day or night his face bore the same placid expression, beyond disappointment or yearning. Never did he seem to be waiting for something, or expecting anything.

"Hey, Hunt."

So much for his disguise.

"Hey, Augie. Want to make some money?"

"How?"

"Surveillance."

"How much?"

"Fifteen an hour. Cents, that is. All the orangeade you want."

"That your best offer?"

"Ice cream, too. When we finish."

"What kind?"

"Whatever you want. Ice pop, Dixie cup, or cone."

"One of each."

"Deal."

Hunt hoisted his shoulders, twined his fingers around the straps to keep the tank secured, and started off. The weight of it forced his neck and shoulders forward as he headed in an uneven line to the beach. When they reached the steps, he handed Augie the thin silver life guard's whistle he'd bartered for. It had cost him two creamsicles and a lemon ice. Not a bad deal, especially in light of the fact the ice cream was on the house. It was the least the Salt Air Concessions Company could spring for, he felt, considering the ordeal he was about to endure.

"Emergency use only," he told Augie. "In case she pops up out of nowhere and you can't get to me in time."

They were heading for the south end first, a trial run. Not many people from their neighborhood hung out there. Mostly folks from the west Bronx. Tougher. Meaner. Or so it seemed. But strangers, at least. No one he knew.

This close to the arcade the beach was crowded: umbrellas, beach blankets, kids running back and forth, radios tuned to WMCA or WINS or WABC with its chime-time bell ringing after every song, the smell of Coppertone heavy as heat in the air. Augie stayed twenty or thirty yards ahead. His head swiveled like a lighthouse beacon guiding ships to a safe passage, or a periscope in search of its target: strawberry blond hair, a body

6

that hadn't yet lost all of its baby fat. That was Debby Ann.

At least ten times Augie raised his hand as though he'd spotted her. False alarms. There were plenty of girls who looked like her, Hunt had to admit, though in *his* mind she was one of a kind. He walked with his head down, not looking left or right. He didn't care if he sold anything or not.

A desert of relatively uninhabited sand opened around them, only a few umbrellas scattered bright as balloons, each with its small oasis of shade. Hunt had to work harder, toiling under the weight of the tank like a pack animal, traveling long distances to his left or right if someone yelled to him for a drink, the sand difficult to push through, the heat rising through his shoes.

In the striped shade of an abandoned lifeguard stand, he unstrapped the tank and glared at it propped on the sand, the silver dome-shaped top reflecting the sun in a vicious blade of light. Paper cups hung from a cylindrical tube attached to the tank. He pulled out a cup, opened the spigot, filled it, and handed it to Augie. "It's mostly sugar, it's watered-down, the flavor's artificial, and it may have hairs in it. Drink at your own risk."

Augie gulped it down. Hunt filled him another.

"You supposed to give it away like this?"

"I'll take it out of my salary. No big deal." He filled a cup for himself, took one sip, made a face, then spit it out. When he removed his hat his hair stuck wet and shiny to his scalp. He combed it out best he could. "I'd quit this in a minute." What he didn't say was that his parents would kill him if he did. He was saving for college. Every little bit helped, as his father too many times had reminded him. "I would," he said, staring past Augie. "I sure as hell would."

A girl walked by with a radio playing the Everly Brothers. *Crying in the Rain.* One of Debby Ann's favorites. Shoulders slumped, Hunt leaned against the stand as if he might give up. "Just my luck she's out here somewhere listening to it right now."

"What number on the charts?" Augie asked. It was a game they played.

At first, Hunt didn't respond. He stared with a stony expression at the blue-grey water that drifted toward Long Island. Then he looked at Augie with a hint of defiance. "32."

"Number 10?"

"Elvis. *Devil in Disguise*. RCA. Up from 26." He had this habit of memorizing the Top Forty Countdown each week by artist, title, label, and change of position on the chart from the previous week. He'd challenge Augie to try to stump him but so far Augie never had.

"Number 39?"

"Johnnie Mathis. *What will Mary Say*. Columbia. Down from 31."

"Number 22?"

"Bobby Vinton. *Blue Velvet*. Epic. First time on the charts." He checked his watch then crouched and slipped his arms through the straps of the tank. When he stepped out of the shade, he groaned.

A white haze lifted from the sand. The thermometer above the arcade read 92 degrees, unusually hot for June. They followed a trail of sound to the north end, radio to radio: *say you're gonna miss me . . . just say you will, say . . . mama said, mama said . . . hey, hey, tonight's the . . . don't leave me, darling . . .for always and ever . . . baby, won't you please. . .* Beachgoers flagged down Hunt with all kinds of names: mister, boy, sir, you, yo, hey, guy, soda man, buddy, Mac, Charlie, Joe, Jake, fellah, captain, boss, young man, muchacho, dipshit, douchebag.

Three more times Augie thought he spotted Debby Ann. Once he even blew the whistle and Hunt dove to his knees like a wounded camel. False alarms again, all three of them. Hunt plodded on stooped like an old man, his face red and slick, sweat stains darkening his shirt under his arms and down his back.

Heading to the north end just past noon, Augie was sure he spotted Debby Ann for real. Section 3, near the lifeguard stand. He blew the whistle—two short blasts—which meant watch out, near and probable danger ahead. Hunt's head popped up while he was dispensing orangeade to some kids. He jerked around in search of an escape route.

Augie moved closer to the suspect. It was Debby Ann, all right. She lay on a blue towel, talking to some guy—Augie saw now it was the meanest guy in the neighborhood, the leader of the Brandos who was always giving him dirty looks, telling him *go back to where you came from, wherever the hell that is.*

Debby Ann was fluffing out her hair with her fingers. She wore a blue and white polka dot two-piece which didn't hide her few extra pounds. But she was cute, Augie had to admit, real cute in that Irish kind of way. Her fair skin had turned blotchy red from the sun, especially across her nose and cheeks.

Augie waved Hunt away but Hunt had already veered off toward the water, making a wide loop around the lifeguard stand. Sales were less likely at the water's edge where it was cooler and people didn't have their wallets but some guy in a Yankees cap yelled, "Hey! Hey, bub!" He held out a dollar but Hunt pulled his safari hat lower, his neck tucked in like a turtle, and charged past him.

"Hey, yo! Hey, yo, numbnuts, I'm talkin' to you." Waving the dollar bill, the man lurched after Hunt for a few steps, then shot him the finger.

Hunt moved so fast Augie had to run to catch up. He crossed into Section 2, and didn't even slow down when he reached the north jetty. He climbed the rocks unsteadily but with determination, then thrust himself forward with a lumbering pitch and roll across a muddy stretch of beach nobody used and finally up an embankment into the picnic area.

In the shadow of the trees he slipped the tank from his shoulders and slumped to the ground. From neck to belt, the back of his shirt was one dark sweat-stain. He sat with his head in his hands, then he stood and scaled his hat at a tree and paced between the picnic tables. "Question is, did she see me or didn't she? I mean, there was some distance between us, right? Seventy-five, eighty feet at least. I had the hat down, I had shades on, I could have been anybody." He stopped pacing and stared hard at Augie. "What do you think? She see me or what?"

Augie thought it over. "Probably not."

"Probably? *Probably?* Probably's not good enough. I have to know. I have to know *definitely*."

Augie thought again, considering the fact that he hadn't yet been paid. "Definitely not."

"You think so?"

"Definitely." Augie eyed him carefully. After a moment he ventured to ask, "Can I have my ice cream now?"

Hunt wasn't listening, staring as he was toward the beach where Debby Ann was no more than a blur at this distance. "So, Augie?"

"Yeah?"

"How do you know? How do you know *definitely*?"

Augie took his time answering. He didn't want to be blamed for not spotting her soon enough. "I just kinda know, I guess."

—3—

All afternoon Hunt tortured himself, refusing to abandon the safety of the picnic grove until he was certain Debby Ann had left the beach. He made Augie re-enact the scene of their near confrontation, detail by detail: had she been looking up or too busy talking? *When* did she look up? *Before* or *after* the whistle blew? Was she facing *toward* the water or *away* from it?

Augie's answers were indirect, if not evasive. He didn't want Hunt to punk out on the deal.

Hunt kept repeating, "And she was with a guy, too," as if the very repetition itself would make it not true. "Kind of big, right? A greaser."

"Yeah. The Brando dude."

What she saw in the guy, Hunt couldn't figure. Except that Sal had a four year football scholarship to Villanova in the fall compared to Hunt's half-scholarship to study English and American Lit at Fordham, so Sal could lounge around the beach all afternoon and talk to girls while he, humble low-life that he was, worked for minimum wage—55 cents an hour—an indentured servant in a free society, at the beck and call of every bather with a thirst and three nickels to slake it.

At the storeroom Big Tony couldn't understand how he'd sold less than a single tank of orangeade. His teeth clamping down on a White Owl panatela, he glared at Hunt suspiciously. "On a day when the temperature tops 90 degrees, on a day when every other Rat out there sells in excess of *five* tankfuls—and that's including two first-timers and two shit-for-brains flunk outs from DeWitt C, the worst high school in the city—you don't sell even one. How you figure that?"

Hunt shrugged, stared at the floor. "Guess they weren't thirsty where I was."

"Oh, yeah?" Big Tony's lips curled tighter around the panatela, mangling it. "Where was that? The moon?"

At home, the bathroom still hazy from the shower to purge the lingering traces of orangeade, the challenge of the night ahead beckoning, he examined himself in the mirror: defect by defect.

The phrase, *he doesn't have his head screwed on straight*, applied literally to *his* head which seemed, in his assessment, to list slightly leftward. Try as he might, he couldn't get it to appear straight without forcing it and even then it appeared a bit off kilter. In its natural state, it maintained a steady inclination to the left.

He thought changing his hair style might help. From infancy, his mother had parted his hair on the right. He was in the process of re-training it by brushing it vigorously to the opposite side. A hundred stroke minimum, morning and night. He worked hard on it now, forcing the stiff bristles against his scalp so forcefully it hurt. Still the strands sprung back, standing at odd, squiggly angles. He settled for rubbing in some Vaseline to flatten them.

His ears were another problem. Too long, he thought, but at least in time he could camouflage their size by letting his hair grow. His shoulders seemed too thin and frail, his chest not developed enough. That spring he'd started lifting weights

12

in hopes that a more manly chest might even things out, deflect attention from the scarcity of flesh covering his bones. Thus far, he had to admit, the results had yet to manifest themselves.

The mirror stopped at his navel so, thank God, he was spared a reflection of what he felt to be his equally inferior lower parts: knobby knees and bony ankles. All in all, he had to concede, his ranking was low on the hipster scale.

He looked to Dean for inspiration. It was the *way* the actor moved, he decided, that added the finishing touches to the man's charm. Slow and laconic. Unhurried. In his eyes an abiding sadness and hurt. And he kept his mouth shut most of the time, let his silences speak for him, let his eyes show the hurt. That made women want to comfort him. Like in *East of Eden*. The way he carried himself, half-stooped over, his sloped shoulders and pleading eyes a monument to his helpless agony—that's what made Julie Harris betray her boyfriend for him. She simply couldn't stop herself.

That was the look he wanted to cultivate. That was the look he would offer to Debby Ann tonight.

He put on his tux—ruffled shirt, white jacket, black pants, bow tie—and shook his head in dismay.

At dinner his father spoke of the threshold Hunt was crossing, how a new world would be opening before him. Oh, to be young again, his father said wistfully and his mother rolled her eyes. She'd baked a yellow cake with chocolate icing, eighteen yellow candles. His aunt and uncle, Josie and Gene, came over to celebrate. Gene had a golf ball-sized growth in the center of his forehead; Hunt wondered why he'd never had it removed but was afraid to ask. Josie had grown heavy over the years and looked nothing like the slim, beautiful woman in the wedding photos Hunt had seen. Once you got married, he concluded, the question of cool went out the window.

When he was leaving, he reminded his father about the arrangement they'd made: that tonight, for the first time, he would be allowed to stay out without curfew. It was the one birthday gift he'd asked for and his parents, after a lengthy period of consideration that transpired over several weeks and after Hunt's assurance he would act responsibly, had finally agreed.

Now his father simply said, "Just don't do anything foolish, as we've discussed." But the look he gave Hunt reached deeper. It said: *We've already lost one son, we can't bear to lose another.*

—*4*—

There was nothing in the Chester Heights housing project that didn't remind Hunt of Toby: the hallways where he was always searching for a place to jump out and surprise Hunt, the chain-like fence along the walkways that he loved to swing from, the grassy lawns where he would practice what he called his tumble-salts, never quite perfecting them, landing awkwardly on his side and giggling. What he particularly loved were the terra-cotta gargoyles that graced the entranceways or hung from the edges of the seven- story buildings: winged angels and delicate nymphs and reclining maidens. "Girls can't fly," he would say and Hunt would explain that these were simply artist's renditions meant to add beauty to the otherwise lackluster brick walls the color of rust, and Toby would laugh thinking Hunt had made a joke.

On his way to the prom he had to cross the Main Oval, a park-like space of trees and grass and flowers at the project's center. He was careful as always to avoid the north end where they used to take Toby to play. Instead he took the center walkway, past the pool and the fountain.

Despite this, Toby found a way to appear. *Standing on a bench, posing for a photo. White shirt, tan shorts. His head*

15

cocked sideways. Making a silly face with wide staring eyes, fingers pulling the corners of his mouth apart.

Hunt turned away, walked faster.

At the end of the avenue, the 177th Street station marked the project's border. Businessmen and women, smartly dressed, traversed the circular plaza beneath the elevated tracks on their return from Manhattan, among them one less fashionably attired, a pole-like bedraggled figure weaving his way through the crowd holding a makeshift cardboard placard in one hand and a plastic cup thrust outward in the other. "Poems for a penny," he called out, holding up the placard and rattling the coins in his cup. "The power of the word for a pittance."

When he spotted Hunt, he came toward him uncharacteristically clear-eyed, reciting his favorite lines from *Oedipus Rex*—for what would have been at least the hundredth time that day—his *verse du jour*:

> *Oh, ohhh—the agony! I am agony—*
> *Where am I going? Where on earth?*
> *Where does all this agony hurl me?*
> *My darkness, drowning, swirling around me*
> *Crashing wave on wave—*
> *The stabbing daggers, stab of memory*
> *Making me insane.*

Hunt, an aspiring writer himself, joined him in the closing couplet of the play: "Count no man happy till he dies, free of pain at last."

"No truer words," the old man said. He removed his homburg and held it to his chest, eyes streaming with inordinate passion. "No truer words."

"Since when, Alphonso, are you passing off Sophocles as your own?"

"The muse abandoned me today, my boy, left me a poor stranded orphan." He waved his hat at the passersby around them. "Dispossessed among the bourgeoisie. The Greek was all I had to offer."

16

"How's business?"

"Occasional."

"Any new revisions?"

The man had been a Dean of the College of Arts and Sciences at NYU before wine and Irish whiskey brought him down. Now he spent his days drinking and peddling his poems, endlessly revised variations of Eliot's "The Hollow Men." They all began this way:

> *We are the Tattered Ones*
> *We are the Tattered Ones*
> *Standing apart*
> *Stuffed with straw like our makeshift mattresses*
> *Our dried voices meaningless*
> *As wind in a subway tunnel. . .*

This last a reference to the very station under which they stood, where along with several other homeless men he'd taken up residence. For a month now, he'd lived under the subway stairs, falling asleep—he liked to say—to the pitter-patter of tired feet traveling to or from the elevated tracks above, the feet of slaves to the world from which he'd been exiled.

"The revision process never ends," he said now, answering Hunt's question over the rumble and screech of the uptown local which had pulled in above them. "It's the closest we poets come to understanding the concept of eternity."

Alphonso lowered his head, his expressive and sober eyes giving way to a dark concern. "Alas, though, greater woes attend us. Our enemies descend."

"Who?"

"The hooligans. The one they call the Butcher. He and his pals paid us a visit in the wee small hours. Trampling us in our bedding, dousing us with their unfinished beer, referring to us in the cruelest and most abject of terms. In short, routing us from a peaceful slumber and making off with various and sundry of our humble possessions."

"Was anyone hurt?"

"Only in the heart's tender places. The issue of our disbanding has been raised. It has been suggested we might do better if we went our separate ways."

Hunt reacted the way he would if the family of one of his friends decided to move away—with sadness and disappointment. Over time he'd gotten to know each of the tattered ones, considered them as friends: Jumbo, the ex-jazz musician; O'Shea, the Irishman who came to the Bronx via Australia first and then the Bowery; Mr. Pee, whose real name or background no one knew, his nickname a consequence of his malfunctioning bladder; and, of course, Alphonso—to whose cup and theirs he had been a reliable contributor each time he crossed beneath the station.

"Won't the police help?"

Alphonso laughed. "Bless your innocent heart." He stroked his grey beard, amused at Hunt's naiveté. "But I didn't mean to trouble you. To each his own. Burdens included."

He ushered Hunt to the stairway beneath which he stored his belongings, rummaged there until he found the spiral notebook that contained the forever incomplete manuscript of his masterpiece, scrawled sometimes in pencil, sometimes in pen, all of it—to Hunt's eye—indecipherable.

"Despite last night's turbulence, I did manage to add a few lines to section 5," he said, reading from a half-written-upon page toward the back of the notebook. "Between the first express at dawn and the last local at midnight, falls the shadow; between the morning papers and the evening, falls the shadow; between the morning feet running and the evening feet plodding, falls the shadow."

He looked at Hunt hopefully. "What do you think?"

"I like it. It's coming along." He dropped fifty cents into the old man's cup. "Keep working on it. I want to hear more tomorrow."

"If there is a tomorrow," Alphonso said. "If we're not all dead by enemy hands."

—5—

Between the conception and the creation, Hunt thought as he walked in the shadow of the el away from the station, recalling his own humble literary efforts: *Between the conception and the creation, falls the shadow*.

The ubiquitous shadow.

He worried that this place, this Bronx of his heritage, would never be worthy of an epic. What was there that could possibly be heroic about prom night, els, souped-up '55 Mercs, greaser Romeo football jocks like Sal the Butcher?

Where was the majesty in the lives around him, including his own, so ordinary, so starved of high tragedy in the classic sense, in the sense that Aristotle defined it: a man who falls from happiness to misery by his own hand, some error of judgment that dooms him? As far as he could tell, he himself did not even meet the minimal standards for a tragic hero: he had no tragic flaw. At least none that he yet knew of.

A squeal of brakes on the street behind him made his breath catch, his body stiffen. When he turned the corner, moving away from the el, he saw Augie sitting on the stoop of 1241 Olmstead, back against the wall, dictionary in hand as he stared toward the street. He wore the same black jersey and black pants from the beach, his Yanks cap tilted left at the same odd angle.

"Hey, Augie. What you looking up?"

"*Obdurate*."

"Why that word?"

"That lawyer guy upstairs. The one who lives on four. He called me that."

"In reference to what?"

"In reference to I'm always sitting out here on the stoop. He says he's told me a hundred times it makes the building look bad. Like a slum. According to him, because I won't cooperate I'm downright stubborn. *Obdurate*."

"Your folks not home yet?"

"No."

"When?"

"Dunno."

There were things to do, preparations to be made to insure a successful encounter with Debby Ann, but Hunt sat beside him on the stoop.

"Word is the Golden Guineas are coming 'round tonight," Augie said.

"Who said that?"

"Some kid. Heard it from his older brother."

"Jeez." The last thing he needed tonight was a gang war.

"They beat on people with their belts."

"I know. I know." Their signature. They wore shiny black belts with a thick metal buckle in the shape of a G. In a matter of months they'd become the Bronx's most feared gang.

Of all nights, he thought. Didn't he have enough on his mind figuring out how to please Debby Ann?

He looked at Augie, trying to read his face wiped clean of expression. "You eat?"

"Yeah."

"You sure?"

"I should know if I ate or not, shouldn't I?"

Hunt reached into his pocket and handed him two dollars. "Thanks for helping me today."

Augie pocketed the bills.

Hunt handed him another fifty cents.

"What's this for?"

"Tip. You really helped me out."

"I don't think she saw you."

"I'll find out soon enough."

"You going to ask her?"

"I'll know by how she looks at me. At the dance. I'll see it in her eyes."

If Augie had an opinion on the matter, he didn't voice it. Hunt's heart raced hard, fueled by dread.

The evening settled around them. Grey light falling like rain from the sky. A few kids rode their bikes up and down the block. A white van idled at the corner and Hunt turned away. Across the street an old man stared from a fifth floor window.

"How come you're not playing your harmonica?"

"Lost it."

"Where?"

"Wouldn't be lost then, would it?"

"I meant, where do you think you lost it?"

Augie shrugged. "The beach, I guess."

"Today? Damn."

"Sand will ruin it. Even if somebody turns it in."

The grey light fell harder around them, bringing with it an unsettling silence. Dusk, Hunt had written in one of his poems, was the cruelest hour. Across the street, the old man in the window kept staring. It was a common sight in the neighborhood, someone staring out the window like that. Mostly older people; they stared the longest. Blank stares, registering nothing.

The white van at the corner moved out into the traffic of the avenue.

Hunt felt the beginnings of the Blue Mood coming on. Usually it was a memory of Toby that brought it on, but it was a feeling that went beyond Toby, too. It was a kind of loneliness so acute he had to give it a special name. A low, empty feeling that changed the world around him, or the way he felt about it, maybe both. It would

21

last anywhere from a few seconds to a few minutes—long enough to undermine the foundation his life was built upon. It seemed to embody all the sorrow the world kept hidden in its soul, and more.

He turned away from the old man at the window and focused on Augie. "You want me to get you an ice cream? An Italian ice?"

"Not really."

"Okay. I guess I'll see ya."

"See ya."

Still, Hunt lingered before walking off.

At the corner store, to assess his financial condition, he spread the folds of his wallet. Never a pretty sight, but tonight it was loaded up with nearly thirty dollars, his week's pay. He'd meant to leave it home so his father could deposit it in his college account as he did every week. But he'd been thinking about Debby Ann and forgot.

He walked to the back of the store where there were 45s for sale and a few used music instruments: a guitar, a ukulele, an accordion and two harmonicas. He bought the better looking of the two harmonicas and brought it back to Augie who took it without saying anything, observing it with a critical eye before testing it out with a few toots. He took a breath and launched into an exaggeratedly mournful version of *Taps*. When he finished he looked at Hunt with a half-smile.

Hunt shook his head. "You've got a strange sense of humor, you know that?"

"'Least I've got one."

"Meaning, I don't?"

"Sometimes you're in a funk."

"Yeah, well, you'll know what it's like when you're older. When you have things on your mind. You're too young now."

"Me? I'm not too young for nothing."

"Anyway I liked it. Your version of *Taps*. Real heartfelt." Hunt laughed, thinking of how he might end up if Sal's interest in Debby Ann continued. "You can play it at my funeral."

—6—

Hunt arrived at the church early, time enough to stop in for a visit; the prom was to be held in the basement below. For reasons of her own, Debby Ann had insisted they meet here rather than at her apartment house. Another in a growing list of bad omens but, not feeling he had any choice, he had acquiesced.

Inside the church, six elderly women waited ahead of him for Confession, their heads—every one of them—bent into hands that held a rosary, the occasional fragmented words of a Hail Mary escaping from quivering lips. Hunt bent his head forward in a prayer of his own: that Debby Ann would greet him with an open smile, free of qualification, that they would have a lot of laughs at the prom and that afterward, some time before the sun rose on a new day, she would declare her love for him.

The confessional line was moving slowly so he went to a side altar to light a candle for Toby. He dropped a dime into the coin slot. Unfortunately, the candle he wanted—the one dead center in the middle row, directly below the statue of St. Helena—was already lit. He believed because of its prominent position it would be the one most noticed by the spirit of the Saint. No sense taking the chance that his petition might be lost among the many tiny flames flickering in the three rows of candle-holders so he reached forward and pinched out the flame of his preferred candle then re-lit it with the taper as he whispered to Toby, the way he used to before bedtime: *no bad dreams tonight, little buddy. May you awake to sunshine filling the windows.*

He added, as an afterthought, a secondary petition. That the Golden Guineas wouldn't invade the neighborhood and ruin his chances with Debby Ann.

When he returned to the confessional, the line had dwindled to one woman ahead of him. She was small and gnome-like, her shoulders and head shaped like a hook pulling her earthward. She was so old that when she took a step her forward motion was imperceptible. When her turn arrived, Hunt held the confessional door open and reached for her hand to guide her forward, a process that unfolded in slow motion, until she was finally inside and he could close the door after her, stepping discreetly back lest he overhear her secrets.

He was feeling vaguely nauseated.

He suspected it was the sacrament of Penance itself, the overwhelming number of sins he had to confess descending upon him with the force of an avalanche: the *jealousy* and *envy* he felt toward Sal the Butcher and really any guy who talked to Debby Ann, particularly those who asked her to dance, *anger* too at her for saying yes; *pride* for thinking he was better than Sal, better than any of the guys who asked her out, pride too for thinking someday he might become a great poet; *sloth* because he didn't work hard enough to make that happen; *lust* because try as he might he couldn't help thinking about Debby Ann in a carnal way; *greed* because he knew an ordinary life would never satisfy him, that he wanted the best of everything this world had to offer. There was not one of the Seven Deadly Sins he wasn't guilty of except, maybe, *gluttony.*

Then he remembered how much he'd stuffed himself last week at Fat Benny's Clam Shack on City Island at their All-You-Can-Eat Friday night Raw Bar.

24

That's what it meant to be a Catholic. You were down on your knees for every little thing, saying how sorry you were. Perfection of the self was more than a goal; it was an expectation. It was always something you were falling short of.

In the basement, the music had begun, a singer whose voice he didn't recognize was screaming *My heart says go, go, go, let's rock let's rock let's rock,* the music cranked up so loud the church floor trembled beneath his feet, totally possessed with the devil's beat. The old lady ahead of him must have died in the confessional, or else her list of sins was longer than his. She'd been in there hours, he thought.

Contrition would have to wait.

Time to dance.

7

Debby Ann's round, pretty face rendered him helpless. She wore a strapless white lace gown, on her head a sparkling silver tiara. He imagined that beneath her eyes, the color of the bluest sea, roiled depths he had yet to discover. Around them, the church basement's drab grey space had been transformed into a crepe-paper wonderland of red and gold streamers and balloons.

"May I have the honor of this dance?" he asked, following Brother Aloysius' instructions. She said neither *yes* nor *no*, she did not take his hand—this a situation for which Brother had not prepared him. So he took her hand tentatively and guided her to the dance floor where, with mechanical rigidity, they executed a modified foxtrot to the Five Satins singing, *In the Still of the Night*.

For the two minute and eighteen second song, his body had never felt so inflexible, so inanimate, his shoulders like lead weights that rendered him nearly immobile. Despite that, he was transported to a higher realm by his proximity to her. Her hair fascinated him, swirled as it was on top, flipped at the base of her neck, a row of bangs decorating her forehead. There was, too, the springtime flowers' smell of her and something more elusive, a pulsing he could feel inside himself: in his fingers where they touched her waist, in the palm of his hand where it met hers, moist and sticky though the contact was. And he could feel the pulsing *out*side as well, in the close air between their faces, their bodies.

In the past when they'd talked, their conversations had been short-lived, abrupt, her minimalist responses to his questions—*yes, no, maybe, a-huh*—occasionally piercing the heavy silence. In response to a more thought-provoking question such as, "What's your favorite book?" or "Which of the Existentialists do you find most interesting?" her replies were of the "I don't know, really" or "I haven't really thought about it" variety.

Now, hoping to begin the evening on a higher plane, he asked her if she thought religion was becoming extinct in the modern world, in light of the fact that recent polls reported fewer people attending church.

She looked at him as if she didn't understand. "*I* go to church."

He told her he thought the truest form of religion were the small acts of kindness human beings did for one another every day. Small blessings, he called them.

To that, she had no reply whatsoever.

He thought perhaps she was insecure, as shy inside as he was, waiting for someone to help her express her inner being. He thought he should say something quickly to cover the awkward silence. "It's my birthday today."

"That's nice."

"Number 18. The big one."

"They'll all be big from now on, I guess."

"Yes," he said but he wasn't sure to what he was agreeing.

When the song ended she forced a smile and walked back to their table, her face blank as a runway model. At least, he thought, she hadn't mentioned the beach. Maybe Augie was right; he'd gone undetected, after all. But watching her chat with her girlfriends, oblivious to his presence and casting frequent glances across the room in Sal the Butcher's direction, he found less comfort than might be expected in that thought.

27

When dinner was served, she barely picked at the Chicken Fricassee and spoke only when spoken to. When he asked if something was wrong, she said, "Like what?"

After the meal she said she wanted to dance with her girlfriends, her code for "other people," so he wandered off on his own. From behind the large squared-off support columns on the basement edge, he couldn't see the dance floor; he didn't have to bear witness to how close she danced with other guys. Sometimes kids came back here to sneak a smoke or chug-a-lug whiskey from those small bottles they served on airplanes; mostly, though, it was where coats were left on the chairs along the wall.

Tonight he had the place to himself. He took out his pocket-sized memo pad, hoping to add a few lines to his epic. He considered titling it, "A Moment in the Day of the Tragic Life of an Outer-Borough Wallflower" but immediately rejected that as too mawkish, too wimpy.

He closed his memo pad and leaned back against the column, absorbed completely now by its shadow, and took refuge in another of his secret identities: the future pre-eminent deejay of the entire New York, New Jersey, Connecticut, tri-state area, five thousand powerful watts broadcasting his voice to millions of his loyal, adoring fans through the long hours of the overnight. And why were they so loyal and devoted? Because he played the music they loved, this music of their youth, their hopes and dreams. Not only the songs they could dance fast to, but the songs that touched their hearts, that reached deep into their loneliness and longing and loss, the beat of his music mimicking the very beat of their hearts.

In between songs he would read their dedications to long-lost girlfriends and boyfriends—*To Bobbie on Tremont Ave who I never forgot. . . .To Diane from Fordham Road, who still is the girl of my dreams. . . .to the dark-haired boy with the beautiful eyes who I saw one morning on the Pelham Parkway bus.* He would be the bridge between past and present, between dreams and reality. His radio name would be the Nite Hawk, the guide of lost souls through the night. He would be the true son of the king of rock n' roll, the undisputed successor to Allen Freed and he would carry Allen's legacy into the future. He would insure that rock n' roll would never die.

A shadow crossed his reverie and when he returned to earth's surface Caroline Longo stood in front of him. "Brooding again?"

"I'm not brooding."

"Prove it."

"How?"

"Dance with me."

He'd known her since first grade. Their mothers were best friends and were always trying to push them together, but Hunt wasn't interested. Caroline was tall and thin and awkward because of her height but on the dance floor—like Hunt, fast dances only—she was cool and graceful as a spinning top. In fact, they'd invented a dance together called the Roddle, an abbreviation of their original name for it which was the Rockin' Waddle—part duck-walk, part shimmy and part Lindy. It showed her off to her best long-legged advantage.

They danced to *Blue Suede Shoes, Whole Lotta Shakin' Goin' On, Hound Dog, Party Doll*, and *See You Later, Alligator*, this last their best dance of the night, Caroline throwing her head back and waving her arms and looking flushed and so happy, his own moves slick as if he had greased ball bearings for joints, but Debby Ann was talking to her girlfriends and didn't notice.

He watched her turn down a few guys, thinking that was a good sign, until she started looking in Sal's direction and he came over, not even having to ask her to dance, Debby without hesitation sliding into his arms. Worse luck, it was the slowest of slow ballads, the Moonglows singing *Ten Commandments of Love*, a make-out song if there ever was one, the two of them barely moving, hugging close.

"Gross," Caroline said from the sidelines where they watched. "Miss Sack of Irish Spuds and Guido the Gangster King. That nose of hers won't look so cute when those freckles turn dark. Look at her. She's already got a double chin."

"No, she doesn't."

29

"Ha! He who has eyes cannot see."

She took his hand and pulled him onto the dance floor, bumping awkwardly against him as they slow-danced, saying "Sorry" again and again. "I guess I'm just too tall to be grace-ful."

"It's me," he said. "I can't slow dance to save my life."

She'd been deliberately standing in a way to block his view of Debby and Sal, her shoulder like a ridge above which Hunt couldn't see. She turned now to get a look at them herself. "Maybe I should dance like potato sack there. Stand in one place like a lump and wiggle my rump."

To Hunt's dismay, Debby and Sal were still standing close, holding hands, though the song had ended. He was feeling ill again. "I have to go to the men's room. Excuse me, okay?"

He went inside a stall, latched the door and leaned against it. He felt weak in the knees and closed his eyes, thinking that might help.

It didn't.

He pulled himself up straight, muttered "Get hold of your-self," one of his father's favorite mantras whenever Hunt got too weighed down with feeling, and lurched out of the stall.

At the sink, washing up, was Norm Blevsky, senior class prankster and object of ridicule, best known for his portrayal of one of the shepherds in the Christmas pageant, wearing nothing under his tunic but a jock strap, a condition he revealed pub-licly the last night of the pageant by flashing the Virgin Mary as she lifted baby Jesus from the crèche and for which he was given six days' suspension.

His other claim to fame was the number of times he'd been rejected asking girls to dance—90 something and counting, ac-cording to his calculation, over the four years of high school. He'd had to resort to a cousin for his prom date.

"Heard the rumor?" he asked.

"The Golden Guineas, you mean?"

"Yeah. You think it's true?"

"I don't know."

"Could be a rumor. Could be true." He seemed to want to debate the issue but Hunt had other things on his mind. "See you at McMann's later," he called as Hunt was leaving. "If the bad guys don't show."

Hunt emerged from the men's room at the same time Sal's girlfriend, Angelina Lanzalotto the Sicilian Princess, emerged from the ladies room. She didn't notice him—he wasn't sure if she even knew who he was—intent as she was on making her entrance, a raised head/raised shoulders kind of stride to the edge of the dance floor where she stopped and stared across the room at Sal who was still carrying on his monosyllabic grunt and groan chit-chat with Debby Ann. He must have felt Angelina's eyes—the darkest, most intense eyes imaginable—piercing the back of his thick skull because he turned and came directly to her, offering her his oafish grin as a form of apology.

Which left Debby Ann, for the moment, free.

Hunt thought better of approaching her. He didn't want to compare the forced half-smile she would give him to the wide-mouthed, teeth-filled, unqualified smile she had bestowed upon Sal.

He watched her dance with several guys, no one he knew, and *then* he asked her to dance. Her smile, as he had feared, was qualified, her lips intent on holding something back; but there was some consolation in the fact that it was a marginally less-qualified smile than earlier. Even though it was the Flamingos singing *I Only Have Eyes for You*, so slow, so moody, so much a lose-yourself-in-the-throes-of-romance kind of song, she held him almost at arms' length. When he tried to pull her closer, he felt resistance in her arms, in the tautness of her shoulders. When the song ended, she made a beeline from the dance floor.

"Why won't you dance with me again?" he asked back at their table which looked as if disaster had struck: bunched napkins, soiled plates, half-finished champagne flutes of Hawaiian Punch, cherries drowning in a river of pink cream in the table's center.

31

Finally she said, "You don't slow dance right."

"What's wrong with the way I dance? Tell me."

She shrugged.

He persisted. "What?"

"You don't hold a girl right."

"Like how? Show me."

"That's not my job."

She stared across the room again, her face sour in the candlelight. It was Sal the Butcher she was gaping at with undisguised yearning. He was dancing with Angelina. When Angelina turned in their direction, Debby Ann's eyes flashed with bitter curses.

An up-tempo song came on and she grabbed Hunt's hand and led him dead center on the dance floor. There she shimmied and boogied her heart out and he kept up with her pretty good, he thought, but when she saw that Sal was paying her no attention, that he'd gone off into a dark corner with Angelina, she stopped her shimmy mid-dance and stormed back to the table.

It was then that the Vision first appeared to him. At least she seemed like a vision, the dark-eyed girl with flowing hair and a loose easy stride crossing in front of him on the dance floor, appearing out of nowhere and disappearing just as quickly into the crowd of dancers. His breath caught and his heart jumped a beat. It was a sensation he'd never felt before, deep and instinctive and sure. The kind of feeling that comes when you're face to face with the truth. His body had been stunned into wakefulness.

If he had not already given his heart to Debby Ann, he would have turned immediately and followed her, invited her to dance. Instead he continued his slow march toward Debby like a prisoner on death row hoping for a reprieve.

She sat in sullen silence until the last dance when, without any visible enthusiasm, she relented. Their dance, like her face, was tightly controlled: a back and forth motion in essentially the same spot, as though they were captives within the dance floor's tiniest kingdom.

32

Taking his cue from James Dean, he tried the silent approach instead of his usual efforts to keep the conversation going. She would sense his brooding silence, so his reasoning went, and be intrigued by it, thereby compelling her to ask him questions, eager as she would be to plumb the depths of his mysteries.

While he awaited such a response, he closed his eyes, allowed his head to drift closer to hers until he could feel the heat between them, but then going no closer, thinking he would build anticipation this way, raise expectations, induce *her* to complete the act, press *her* head to his.

Of course this didn't happen.

Their heads made no contact.

Nor did his brooding silence make her curious.

They simply danced without speaking.

So he listened to the words of the song, adding some of his own to better express what he was feeling: *may the incredible, the impossible, may. . . .* He didn't finish. Instead he imagined how thrilling a kiss from her would be.

He thought if he concentrated hard enough on the image of their kiss he could, by the strength of his will, make her see it and feel it as well. But what she said was, "We can stop now. The song's over."

Over her shoulder he saw the Vision again, this time standing alone on the far side of the dance floor. She was getting ready to leave. Blue cotton dress, pale skin, long flowing hair, eyes wide and expectant but a face that registered neither pleasure nor pain. For a moment her eyes met his—they cut through him to a place inside himself he didn't know existed—before she turned and moved with an easy graceful stride toward the exit.

When he looked again at Debby Ann, he saw tears in her eyes. He turned to see Sal about to leave with Angelina on his arm, but not before Sal cast him a murderously brutal glance.

On the staircase, the air thick with perspiration and perfume, they were jostled by the bodies around them; but, once outside, the crowd dispersed quickly. The area in front of the church steps had already thinned out. One of the Brandos—a squinty-eyed guy named Rudy—drew heavily on a cigarette, his steely glance passing over the remaining crowd and fixing itself on Debby Ann and Hunt.

It was not a welcoming look.

Debby made a point to wave at Rudy as she snuggled closer to Hunt.

Across the street, passing beneath the light of a street lamp, he saw the girl in the blue cotton dress. She was walking ahead of her date—some guy Hunt had never seen before—moving quickly and with purpose past the dawdling, kissing couples around her.

A moment later, when he looked again, she was gone.

—8—

The three couples with whom Hunt and Debby Ann shared a limo wanted to keep the party going, so they continued with the night's plan. They bought two six packs of Rheingold and took the ferry to Staten Island. A chance to make out on the upper deck, soft breeze blowing off the water, a full moon (if you were lucky) overhead. That night they *were* lucky, except for Hunt, of course. Debby Ann said she didn't feel well so they sat *in*side, on the hot and cramped lower level, while the Skyliners sang, *Since I Don't have You*, over the P.A.

"It's not fair," he said. "Going with me to make Sal jealous. You've been using me."

"So?"

"It's not right. It's not ethical."

"You're using *me*, aren't you?"

"How? How am I using you?"

She shrugged.

"*How?*"

"Some way," she said. "You just haven't figured it out yet."

It was their longest conversation of the night.

And one that drove him to introspection. Surely, he

thought, she must have been hurt badly in the past to think that love could be reduced to a matter of two people using one another. He didn't know how to show her that wasn't true, not true at all.

Their last stop, before heading back to the Bronx, was a dive bar called Sammy's Bowery Follies. The limo driver recommended it. "Real New York. So seedy it's hip," he told them. "The regulars, they don't know what sober means. *Drinking's* their religion. They worship it day and night." He winked into the rear-view mirror. "No I.D. required."

It was a beer and shot joint, no frills. Down an alley and down five steps to the basement level. Sawdust on the floor. Old timers at the bar hunched over their drinks or passed out with their heads lolling on the dark scarred wood, the room lit only by neon beer signs and the liquid pink/orange glow of the jukebox. When Debby Ann complained it was too dark to see anything clearly, the barkeep said that was the point.

At a long table near the bar Hunt guzzled a beer, drifting inward. Nothing else to do, since Debby Ann was turned away gabbing with one of the other girls. So when a shadow detached itself from the bar and stood before him, muttering something, he had to blink to clear his vision. "Excuse me?" he said.

"You wanna dance with me." It was a statement, not a question.

In the murky light, he could see the woman more vividly now. Grey, wrinkled face. Missing teeth, crooked smile. Hair, too long for a woman her age, falling in frizzy orange curls. Her gold dress, with its sequins and stains, as old as she was.

"No, I—"

"Come on, kid. One dance. It ain't gonna kill ya." Whiskey raged in her eyes but something else, too. Later he would think maybe it was the anger born of defeat, but he couldn't be sure of that, either.

He stood up slowly, half-expecting and hoping she would

36

leave him alone, but she took his hand and drew him toward the jukebox. It was a rough, calloused hand with ragged nails, and though he flexed his fingers to loosen its grip she wouldn't let him go.

Up close, her breath was thick with alcohol, her wrinkles even more pronounced as if they had been engraved in stone. Her lipstick, recently applied and overflowing the boundaries of her lips, left a bright red smear on her chin. He tried to lean away from her, from her whiskey breath and the aggressively floral scent of her perfume, but she clung to him as if she might stumble without him and, overcoming his discomfort, he tightened his grip on her so that she wouldn't fall.

"Just hold me, kid," she murmured. "Sweet and gentle like a baby."

It was all the beer he'd drunk, he explained to himself later, and his heartbreak over Debby Ann. There was nothing left to prove. So he let himself relax, holding her in a long embrace, barely moving, an easy swaying motion to Satchmo on the jukebox singing about a kiss to build a dream on. The woman rested her head against his and closed her eyes. He closed his eyes, too. The soft current of the music carried him. He *let* the music carry him.

When the song ended, the woman's eyes fluttered open. She seemed for a moment not to know where she was, or who this young man was who held her. The smile that broke on her lips was one of embarrassment, of a young girl's shyness.

She offered him a half-curtsy, unsteady and awkward. "Thank you, kind sir."

She turned, her step uneven but determined, as she made her way back to the bar.

When he started back to his seat, he saw Debby Ann watching him. The expression on her face he hadn't seen before. Curiosity for sure, a hint of how-could-you-dance-with-someone-like-*that*, and something more: begrudging admiration, perhaps. He had finally done something to impress her. In the easy grace of his body's motion, in the way he held the old woman with a carefree, languid concern, he had finally learned to slow dance.

Maybe, he thought, there was still a way to win her love this night.

—9—

It was exactly—well, more or less exactly, depending upon the length of one's stride—one thousand two hundred and twenty-six steps from the church where the limo dropped them to Debby Ann's apartment building in Chester Heights. Which translated to three hundred six and a half steps per block. Hunt had traversed the route several times to be certain. Leaving nothing to chance, he had pre-determined his end of the conversation.

First block: talk about the prom. Something funny or weird or noteworthy that happened. Backup plan, if necessary: what rotten weather they'd been having lately. Too hot for this early in the summer.

Second block: talk about plans for the summer. What is she doing? Where is she going on vacation? Say something exciting and intriguing about *his* plans.

Third block: talk about plans for the Fall. College? Job? Goals?

Fourth block: talk about the future *beyond* college. Hopes and dreams. The long range. All right to be philosophic and poetic, but not extravagantly so. Be cool.

They crossed the street alongside the church, past the Park Abbey funeral home with a tavern on either side of it, past Sam's candy store and onto the broad avenue between the buildings of Chester Heights. He walked close to her but not too close. He kept looking at her, seeking eye contact, but she walked with her head bent slightly forward, eyes straight ahead.

The first block was easy. Plenty to talk about what with the rumors of a Golden Guineas' onslaught. Did she think they would really come? Was she afraid?

She shrugged. "They want to fight. They don't come after girls."

"But they could." He wanted her to feel unsafe. He wanted her to think of him as her protector.

"They don't come into Chester Heights. They usually stay on the edges, Westchester Ave or Castle Hill or Tremont."

"But they *could*." He straightened his shoulders, stood tall, hoping to suggest he was up to the task of defender.

She didn't seem to be thinking much about it, one way or the other.

He asked, "What are you doing this summer?"

"Summer school." She grimaced. "I failed history."

"Too bad."

"It's *horrible*."

"Least you'll be able to go the beach on your days off." He wanted to see if his mention of the beach triggered a reaction to the afternoon's fiasco.

"It's *so* boring. All those dates and things. All those people to remember. And it all happened so long ago. Who cares?"

"We can learn a lot from the mistakes of the past."

She gave him a funny look. "Not really. Things were different then. Not like now. Not like modern times."

He was thinking even though they didn't agree, things were going pretty well, considering. The conversation even had some flow to it, and she had more than her usual monosyllabic responses to offer.

With that line of reasoning, though, he jinxed himself. "What else will you be doing this summer, fun-wise?"

"Nothing."

"Nothing?"

"I mean it's personal."

When he introduced the topic of what she would be doing in the fall, she climbed another notch on the muteness scale.

"Job, I guess."

"Doing what?"

"Something."

"I'll be going to Fordham."

"Oh."

"Majoring in English."

"Oh."

The last block was approaching and here she shifted even higher on the scale when he asked, "What do you think your future will be like? I mean, eventually. In the future."

"Get married."

"That's it?"

"Have kids."

"And—?"

She gave him the funny look again. "What else is there?"

There were still another hundred yards to her building so he strove for a grand finale. "I've got big dreams. I want to be a writer. Like the Beats."

"Who?"

"You know. Ginsberg, Kerouac, Ferlinghetti. You've heard of them, right?"

"No."

Here, he thought, was the opportunity he'd been seeking: to expand her horizons, to introduce her to worlds she hadn't yet discovered. "They're these really cool writers. Free spirits. They travel around the country in search of adventure. Experience, too—with a capital E. They take these mad non-stop road trips, coast to coast, New York to Florida, all over, here there and everywhere."

"It must be tiring," she said.

"Just the opposite. It energizes them. Makes them want more. Life feeding life, you know?" He waited before adding:

"I'd like to travel around like that. Talk to people. See how they live. Understand what they think."

She gave him a blank look. "Why?"

"I think it would be interesting. Like tonight. At Sammy's. Seeing the people there. How they live."

"I thought it was depressing. I'd rather not know about things like that."

"Like what?"

"Depressing things."

"It's a way to understand us. I mean, not only as a species, but as individuals. You know? It will make me a better person. A better writer, too. " He threw in, as casually as he could, "We could take trips, the two of us. Once I get a car, of course."

Her head seemed bent forward at an even greater angle. She was walking fast. He had to increase his pace to keep up.

At least, he thought, he'd avoided talking about how damn hot it's been.

A white van came screeching up the avenue and his heart tightened in his chest before he turned away, fast. He locked his mind down, tried to steady his breathing.

In front of her building, under a terracotta panel depicting a woman with long curly hair and the body of lion, a group of guys were hanging out, grey shadows against the darker shadow of the brick wall. His first thought was that maybe it was Sal and the Brandos or one of her previous boyfriends like mean-ass Larry Sheehan waiting to fight him. But it was only some public school kids he didn't know except by sight.

In the elevator she stood close to the door, her eyes following the light moving number to number as they climbed to the seventh floor. When the door opened, she bolted through, moving with determination down the hall.

He wanted to kiss her so much but he knew you couldn't simply launch into a kiss. Something had to lead to it, a prelude, a preface, a set-up. Some form of intimacy: a word, a look, a gesture. If he were smarter, he thought, he could think of a clever comment. If he were funnier, he could break the ice with a joke.

42

If he were cooler, he could use his body language or the soulful look in his eyes.

She was almost at her door, almost out of his reach forever.

Do something.

Say something.

In front of her door she turned, her face—despite its cute and coy appeal—as bland and colorless as the beige of the hallway walls.

Say something.

"I'm going to preserve these memories," he blurted out. "I'm going to keep them alive. Not only as a writer. I'm going to be a deejay, too, and play our songs over and over on the radio, and I'm going to end each show with *Try the Impossible*, for you, for us—"

She stared at him, without blinking.

"You'll see. You'll see." It was a promise he was making, to himself as much as to her.

He looked for something in her eyes, her face, the position of her body—*any*thing to serve as a bridge to what would come next.

She was still there. She hadn't yet turned to open her door.

That was his best, his *only*, justification. But it wasn't enough, he knew. He would be taking a one-in-a-million chance.

He leaned forward to kiss her. She drew back and stood stiffly against the door. The blue sea eyes he adored so much were flat, without depth of any kind.

"I don't think so," she said.

Her face was a closed door.

Then, as she slipped inside, there was an apartment door between them, as well.

PART TWO

IN THE STILL OF THE NIGHT

Hunt sat on a bench hunched forward, head down, hands clasped between his knees. With their imposing walls of windows, the buildings that surrounded the small oval where he grieved brooded over him like a judgment.

It felt as if the entire neighborhood bore witness to his rejection.

A lone figure entered the far end of the oval, a shadow assuming recognizable form as it came into the blue-grey light of the street lamps. "The Honorable John James Reardon the Third," it said, "seeking a word with your Highness."

"His Highness grants said request." Hunt slid over on the bench to make room but Johnnie Jay stood looking down at him, sly grin in place, mischief running rampant in his eyes.

"So where's her ladyship?"

"Locked in her castle."

"For the night?"

"Forever."

"Forever?"

"Permanently, yes. Forever."

"Uh-oh." With great solemnity, Johnnie Jay sat down beside him. He was taller than Hunt, his dark hair longer, curlier. "When did it happen?"

"Few minutes ago."

"Here?"

"In her hallway."

"Witnesses?"

"No."

"Thank God for that." Public humiliation was his gravest fear. "Least it didn't happen during the prom."

Hunt gave him a puzzled look.

"You got to keep the dream alive a little longer."

"Small consolation."

"Hey, man, comfort's hard to come by. In this world, you take it where you can get it, *when* you can get it. That's what my old man says. He also says, 'It's a great life if you don't weaken.'"

"Yeah? So?"

"You're weakening."

"I can't help it."

Johnnie Jay shook his head in disapproval. "You think *you've* got it bad. At least you *went* to the prom."

"You could have asked plenty of girls."

"Who?"

"Marianne Ritelli. Joanne O'Brien. Veronica Essler."

"No sexual relevance."

"There are other things."

"Yeah? Name one."

Hunt thought a moment. "Just because I can't think of anything right now doesn't mean it doesn't exist."

"Yeah, yeah."

"You've got an inferiority complex, that's all."

"Takes one to know one." Johnnie Jay grinned. "Hey, I've been using my hand so long it gets jealous the minute I start *talking* to a girl."

Hunt fell silent.

He stared into the dimly lit oval. *Toby stood on one of the*

48

benches, watching him. They would stop here on their way to getting ice cream, the little guy running on the benches, jumping from one to another, Hunt standing close to catch him before he fell.

In Chester Heights, you spent your life in little ovals. He'd seen photos of his mother sitting in one just like this, his infant self tucked in under the foldable vinyl top of a baby carriage. Later it was hopscotch played on a diagram chalked into the pavement; later still there were punch ball games after school and on weekends, a home run if the pink Spalding cleared the green metal fence of the perimeter. Years from now, if he still lived here, he'd be sitting around with the other old men who gathered in the afternoon talking about last night's Yankee game, a cane in one hand and in the other a thermos of coffee. Right now, though, it was a section of barren asphalt—a place where Toby had once played—lit by an eerie blue light, a place to wait while you were pulling yourself together.

"It's my birthday," he said. "I should be celebrating."

Johnnie Jay held up his father's car keys, twiddling his fingers enough to make the metal tinkle. "So let's celebrate. Let's let the old Olds be our wings."

"Thought you had to study tonight."

"I did. I do." He was taking an advanced placement course that would get him into the Honors program at CCNY. All through high school they'd competed for the highest academic rank in their class. Senior year, they ended up in a tie.

"So what does that mean? You finished your homework?"

The sly grin returned. "My parents think so. Hence, the keys." He was standing up now, a nervous twitch in his legs as he paced along the bench. His step was uneven, due—he insisted—to a half-inch discrepancy in the length of his legs and not—as Hunt maintained—to the multitudinous discrepancies of his mental state. "It's still early. Let's open ourselves to the night."

Hunt was thinking there was so much he didn't under-

49

stand. About love. About himself. About his tangled feelings for Toby. So much he wanted to learn.

Johnnie Jay gave him an encouraging look. "Well?"

—11—

The plan was to walk on the beach first—to clear their heads—then celebrate Hunt's birthday and new legal drinking status by bar-hopping at their favorite dance clubs, finishing up at McMann's on Castle Hill where all the neighborhood kids ended their night.

At the beach Johnnie Jay pulled into the parking lot as a dozen choppers—idling at the far end—fired up and, caravan-style, in a thunderous explosion of engine noise and hooting and hollering, roared past them. The leather-vested riders each had the words GOLDEN GUINEAS stenciled high across their backs.

They watched the caravan reach the exit and turn onto the road to City Island, red tail lights shrinking in size, vanishing behind a wall of trees.

Hunt told Johnnie Jay of the rumors.

"Chester Heights? Tonight?"

"That's the word."

"You see those photos in the paper last week?"

The Golden Guineas had taken on a gang from Harlem, the Black Devils. Both the *News* and the *Mirror* had run front page photos: faces, bodies cut and bruised and bloodied by switchblades, baseball bats, chains. It had made Hunt's blood run cold. But there was a positive side to *every*thing, he was thinking now, if you looked hard enough. If it happened tonight in Chester Heights, at least it would no longer ruin his date with Debby Ann. In that sense, his prayer had been answered.

When they reached the stone promenade they saw what the gang had left behind: four benches, or what was left of them, hacked into pieces. No one would be sitting on them anytime soon.

On the sand, here and there, a pair of shadows huddled. A radio played something by the Harptones or the Dells. At this distance, Hunt couldn't tell. And somewhere in the dark a man was laughing. A deep-throated, hearty laugh that went on and on.

He liked the beach at night so much more than the day. Like a church, it was at its best without a lot of people mucking up the mood. He considered telling Johnnie Jay the near disaster he avoided that afternoon but then what did it matter now?

Beside him, Johnnie Jay kept his own counsel. It was the same reverence he would show at a funeral. Grief couldn't be rushed. It passeth at its own pace. He'd read that somewhere— in the Bible, he thought. How else to account for the antiquated form of the verb. In any case he knew people needed peace and quiet to heal. They needed time.

He would give Hunt another fifteen minutes.

They drove to the opposite end of the parking lot where a few cars nosed into the weeds, facing a lagoon.

"You sure you want to be here?" Johnnie Jay asked. He shut down the engine. Darkness rushed at them where the lights had been. Insects chirred. Car metal ticked. They came here usually with a six pack, sat on the car hood and drank and told jokes and stared into blackness, either the sky or the water. Around them, in the other cars, lovers did what lovers do.

Tonight though, Johnnie Jay was well aware, the lad needed plucking from somber thoughts. "Remember that night the guy's girlfriend was freezing him out and he ran out of the car without his pants and into the lagoon, holding his crotch and shouting, 'I've got the worst case of the blue blues in the history of mankind. It's so bad I'm gonna drown myself, I can't take it anymore, I'm gonna drown myself. They hurt so bad, ohhh-hhh, they hurt so bad, oh, oh, ohhhhhh—' And all the cars are honking their horns and flashing their lights till his girlfriend finally comes out looking all apologetic and goes into the lagoon to bring him back, the two of them looking like drowned rats but the guy at least looking like the happiest drowned rat ever, now that things were looking up."

"Wasn't that the night you came up with the idea for the BBBF Society?"

"It was indeed. Banish Blue Balls Forever. As worthy a cause as any for the only club that would have me."

"A club with no plan of action, as I recall."

"Alas, so true." Johnnie Jay glanced at the line of cars facing the lagoon, dark with the secrets of love. "Kind of like rubbing it in our faces, though, isn't it?"

"What is?"

"Coming here."

"Maybe we like to know love exists, even if it isn't ours."

"You think so?"

"I don't know."

"Why do we do the things we do?" He glanced at Hunt who stared beyond the weeds at the slow drift of the lagoon water, blacker than the trees beyond it; and beyond the trees in the far distance the window-lit walls of Chester Heights lifted into the night sky.

"You're right, you know," Hunt said.

"I am?"

"Losing the dream hurts as much as losing the person."

"That's my point. Let's find you a new dream." Johnnie Jay shoved his hand down hard on the horn and shadows moved inside the cars around them, tail lights flared, a few engines fired up.

He swung the Olds sharply over the rutted dirt, the swamp blurring red around them as they jolted past the agitated cars and onto the paved road while Hunt, flinging his bow tie and tux jacket into the back seat, watched the dark line of the lagoon race along with them.

—12—

At the Ship Ahoy, a down and out bar under the el, Hunt ordered his first legal drink. Standing tall at the bar he felt the way he did the first time his Uncle Gene came to the house and shook his hand instead of patting his back or roughing up his hair.

It was a rough and tumble place, murky with shadows, the scarred wood of the ancient bar testament to the scarred and damaged lives of the older men who hung out there, smoking Chesterfields and Camels and Lucky Strikes, hoisting their beers to wash away the burn of the cheap whiskey they downed, shot after determined shot. The walls, what you could see of them, were adorned with fishnets, ship wheels and various other maritime accessories. But despite its noir-ish gloom, its pall of failed hopes and dreams, it seemed to Hunt ripe with possibility. And that was because of the many Irish domestics who sat at small round tables near the bar, waiting to be noticed.

Johnnie Jay said he was itching to try his luck.

His strategy was to build up some confidence with the domestics first, before approaching the college girls who hung out in the back room where there was a jukebox and a dance floor.

So, without wasting any time, he asked one of the domestics to dance. She was thin, had pale skin, a plain face and limp brown hair. With his shoulders thrust upward, he winked at Hunt as he passed the bar, leaning close to say, "God helps those who etcetera, etcetera, etcetera," before following her with his uneven walk into the back room.

The music on the jukebox was mostly from the 40s, big bands like Benny Goodman and the Dorseys and Glenn Miller, the kind of music Brother Aloysius would have approved of. At least, Hunt was thinking, it didn't remind him of Debby Ann.

An old man next to him asked if he had a light. Hunt shook his head.

"You kids," the man said as if Hunt was to blame for something.

When Johnnie Jay returned from the dance floor he seemed flushed and excited. "I'm ready."

"For what?"

"The coeds in back. I'll do all the work. Just follow me."

He lurched into the back room, Hunt a wary several steps behind. No hesitation, though, on Johnnie Jay's part. He went right for the nearest table of five girls. Cute faces, nylon blouses, plaid skirts. He asked the one at the end of the table to dance but she said, "No, thank you, I'm here with my girlfriends."

That sent Hunt skidding into defensive mode but Johnnie Jay, undeterred, rallied to the cause. "Well, then, how about a group thing?" He began pulling her up, her head swiveling back in panic to her schoolmates who, in sympathy, got up one by one and joined her on the dance floor.

So there they were, Hunt and Johnnie Jay, dancing with five college girls to *In the Mood*, taking turns swinging them out and reeling them in, the girls giddy as they twirled, skirts rising. What Johnnie Jay lacked in finesse, he made up for with enthusiasm and of course Hunt, once he let the music take him, showed off his fast dance expertise to more than a few *oohs* and *ahhs*. When the song ended they were all red-cheeked and breathless and he was thinking you'd have to be dead not to feel good when *In the Mood* was playing, outdated though it might be.

Johnnie Jay asked the girls if they could join them but one of them said loudly and firmly, "We're expecting our boyfriends any minute now," so Hunt led the way promptly back to the bar and the comfort of a second round of beers.

Johnnie Jay's strategy was to focus exclusively now on the domestics. They'd been turned down so publicly in the back they wouldn't have a chance in hell with the other college girls who'd witnessed it. First rule of the game: you had to operate from a position of strength. Defeat begat defeat.

While Hunt tried to look cool standing at the bar, Johnnie Jay danced with one domestic after another. Most were in their late teens or early twenties. They wore little or no make-up, plain cotton dresses, their hair hanging straight to their shoulders or curled in at the ends below their jaw lines. Their names were either Mary or Margaret or Maureen. To a greater or lesser degree, they all spoke with an Irish brogue.

In every way, Hunt concluded, they seemed strangers. They wouldn't be going to college, they cleaned houses or took care of someone else's kids, their lives were laid out for them in what Hunt thought of as an ominous example of pre-destination. They would go from one domestic situation to another until, presumably, they'd become their own domestic in their own household.

One thing he *could* say on their behalf, though, was that they rarely ever turned down an offer to dance. Even one from the old grizzled guys at the bar. They were polite and agreeable and would even dance close without much coaxing.

Johnnie Jay was beside him now, urging him to make a move. "You know what they say, don't you?"

"No, what?"

"It's a great life, if you don't weaken."

So Hunt asked the thin girl with the limp hair to dance. She had a perfect record so far. He hadn't seen her turn down one guy who asked her. Not one. So when he approached her she didn't even say *yes*. She simply stood up and followed him to the back room where she slipped obediently into his arms, dancing close to him without any encouragement.

Every person whose path you cross teaches you something. He'd read that somewhere and he reminded himself of it.

Her name was Mary and she worked at a large estate that faced onto a golf course. Three other domestics worked there as well. It was, she said proudly, considered to be the best house to work for in all of Westchester County.

"What do you do?"

"Tidy up, this and that. Being I'm the youngest, the newest, I do what the others have no mind to. Bathrooms, kitchen. Sometimes they let me be nanny to one of the wee ones. I love the wee ones. That's really what I fancy, being a nanny. It takes time though, you see. Till they trust you."

"Yes," Hunt said, but he couldn't think of a follow-up question so he moved slowly with her in silence, listening to the words of the song, *I Don't Stand a Ghost of a Chance with You.* He liked the phrase, *ghost of a chance.*

His mind sought distraction in the decor: framed paintings of sailing ships, fish nets hung across the walls, buoys and anchors hanging from the ceiling. It didn't make any sense, really. There were no sailors here. They were nowhere near dockside, miles from any marina.

Finally he said, "Does all this stuff make you think of the Irish Sea?"

"What stuff?"

"The nets and buoys. The anchors."

"Oh, that. I pay it no mind."

The song ended. The piano version of *Misty* came over the jukebox, painfully soft and tender with yearning.

Mary made no attempt to move away, staying close to him, moving even closer he thought, pressing her head firmly against his so that he could smell her lavender perfume. Through his shirt he could feel the muted—*fragile*—beating of her heart. She was so thin and delicate he thought she might break if he held her too tight or if he moved too quickly.

58

It's a sad world, he was thinking to himself, but somehow he must have spoken the words aloud because she said, "Not so much. I miss my mum but I fancy it here in America. Worst of it is how it gets to one's knees." When she saw he didn't understand, she added: "The floors. Scrubbing 'em."

"Oh."

"I fancy it here better than Ireland. More than a wee bit better."

"That's good," he said. But it still made him feel bleak. This girl thin as air, so far from home, on her knees in some strange family's bathroom.

The song didn't help, either. It was like all the loneliness in the world was locked up in the notes of the piano, straining to be released. All the makings, he was thinking, for a Blue Mood of the deepest kind.

But the song ended and, for the moment, he was spared.

She still held him. It seemed she wouldn't let go.

He disengaged himself gently, said, "It was a pleasure dancing with you, Mary, but I have to get back."

The way she said, "I understand," using it as a barrier to conceal her disappointment, made him feel even worse.

He walked her back to her table and excused himself, taking his position again among the shadows at the bar.

There seemed no point in staying on. If he stayed he imagined he would become—aware neither of the passage of time nor the transformation that accompanied it—one of the older men around him at the bar, looking back across the years for better times, for an explanation of why his life had turned out as it did.

After a few more dances with a tall girl named Margaret who had at least three inches on him, Johnnie Jay joined him at the bar.

He concurred with the futility of it all. "She was ready," he said. "Couple more dances and me and Margie could have been out in the parking lot, but—"

What was left unsaid was everything Hunt already knew, having listened time and again to Johnnie Jay's everlasting lament, usually later in the night than this, usually after many more beers.

They might be driving home from one of their watering holes or sitting on a bench in one of the Chester Heights' ovals, or standing like this at some rough-edged, nicked and scarred slab of wood in the dive-iest of dive bars. No matter the place, the story remained the same. What Johnnie Jay liked to call his story untold. In truth, of course, it had been told countless times and would be told countless times more until the story had an ending that satisfied him.

It wasn't pale, freckle-faced Celtic girls he desired.

No way. No day.

They reminded him too much of his aunts and his cousins. What he wanted was a dark-haired, dark-eyed exotic of European heritage.

Angelina Lanzalotto, to be exact.

He had been adoring her since she moved here in sixth grade. He would adore her until his dying day. With his dying breath.

Until she returned his adoration with an adoration of her own.

Johnnie Jay would then roll his eyes and laugh.

They both knew what the chances were for that.

—13—

Johnnie Jay raised the question: "Does your Low-ness wish to indulge his gustatory instincts before rejoining our brethren at the Rat?" The domestics, he liked to say, were a warm-up for greater glory.

They were standing outside the Ship Ahoy, this section of street under the el dimly lit, deserted.

"He does indeed," Hunt said. "Does *your* Low-ness?"

"Your Low-ness does, as well."

"Let us go then, you and I—" Hunt said, quoting Eliot.

Johnnie Jay joined him without losing a beat. ". . .through certain half-deserted streets, the muttering retreats of restless nights in one-night cheap hotels. . . ."

They raised their voices in unison, inflected with a greater sense of urgency and an even more ritualized and solemn passion. "I have watched the smoke that rises from the pipes of lonely men in shirt-sleeves, leaning out of windows. . . ."

They passed darkened storefronts, moving toward the only other light on the street, spilling onto the sidewalk ahead.

"And the streets," Hunt said, quoting again, "that follow like a tedious argument of insidious intent, to lead you to an overwhelming question. . . .”

“Ham and Swiss?” Johnnie Jay asked. “Or ham and American?”

They stood before the deli counter, laughing.

“Decisions. Decisions,” Hunt lamented. “Mustard or Mayo?”

“White or rye?”

Then they spoke in chorus. “Tomatoes, onions *and* pickle.”

The man standing behind the counter was unamused. He was bearded, Middle-Eastern, weary. It had been a long day. “You again.”

“Amir, who else comes this late at night to keep you company?” Johnnie Jay said. “We’re here as brethren in arms, bearing the fellowship of nocturnal sojourners. You should be happy to see us.”

“Why you stay out so late? Waste time, waste money.”

“This is our pre-combat ritual,” Johnnie Jay explained.

“You talk crazy.”

“You know, the ancient warriors performed *all kinds* of rites to toughen their skin prior to going into battle. They bathed themselves in scalding water, they flagellated themselves, they even soaked in a tub of their own urine. They believed that uric acid strengthened the molecules of the skin, made it harder to penetrate.”

“You crazy man, you know that?”

“This is just our own personal rite, having one of your sandwiches, before doing battle with the ladies of the parish. That’s why we come here. Nothing in our humble neighborhood compares to your delectables. Praise be to Allah.”

“Allah. You know nothing of Allah. You should have more respect. Why you out so late?”

Johnnie Jay laughed. “Amir, it’s only midnight. In America we say, *the night is young.*”

“Why you not home studying?”

“In America we don’t go to school in the summer. In

America summer is for fun."

"In America. In America. In America everything is for fun."

Johnnie Jay hooted. "You got a problem with that, my man?"

"No problem for me. Problem for you."

"Our only problem right now is how hungry we are. What's it going to be, Mr. Hunter?"

Hunt let his eyes roam across the possibilities. Blood-red roast beef, a half–carved turkey breast, a pork roast, three kinds of baked ham, two kinds of salami, bright pink bologna, a slab of bright yellow American cheese and a wheel of pale Vermont cheddar. On the bottom shelf the salads. Macaroni. Potato. Tomato and cucumber and onion. Tuna. Chicken. Shrimp. Egg.

He ordered a ham and Swiss on a hard roll with mayo. Johnnie Jay ordered a ham and American on rye with mustard, mayo, *and* catsup.

"You're a strange boy," Amir said.

Johnnie Jay took that as a compliment.

In the car Hunt asked him to turn on the heater.

"It's eighty degrees out."

"I know. I know. Just do it, okay?" He held his sandwich against one of the vents to warm it, melt the cheese a little. Savoring each bite, he ate the sandwich slowly, taking comfort where he could.

When Hunt finished, he said, "Is it true? About the urine baths?"

"I don't know. Sounded good at the time, though, didn't it?"

On the drive to the Rat, Johnnie Jay showed off his latest feat, steering the Olds with only his pinky finger. He had it wrapped around the lower portion of the wheel—so much cooler that way, he maintained—and he showed how he could swing the wheel easily to the left or right.

"It's a mighty little bugger, the pinky," he said, wiggling it on the rim, "if you take the time to develop it. Most people

63

choose to ignore it and the many fine functions it can perform. A pity, don't you think?"

"I hadn't really thought about it."

"You should. You should think about it. It's the small, seemingly insignificant things that bring joy and wonder into our lives."

"Is that one of your father's sayings, too?"

"All mine." He beamed proudly.

Hunt remembered when Johnnie Jay first learned to drive. His father had insisted he do it by the book. Both hands on the wheel at all times, firmly, at ten o'clock and two. That had been modified quickly, in his father's absence, to a single hand at the two o'clock position, and then modified again to a single hand low on the wheel. And now this, a lone finger, the weakest finger of them all.

Maybe that was how all of life progressed, he thought. You begin with elaborate, established rules then whittle them down to fit your fancy. We were all anarchists at heart.

"Look at this," Johnnie Jay was saying. "I'm working on the left pinky now." He had his left pinky positioned where the right had been. When he tried to turn the wheel, it slipped out of his grip, the car veering into the oncoming lane and heading straight toward one of the stanchions of the el before he grabbed the wheel with both hands to regain control.

"One hand," Hunt shouted. "One full hand minimum or I get out and walk."

Johnnie Jay acquiesced. His right hand, low on the wheel, took over, kept them—for the time being, at least—safely on their side of the road.

—14—

"The Butcher's looking for you."

The announcement came from their classmate Kevin Flanagan, he of the facial acne explosion, outside the Rat.

"What for?" Hunt asked.

"Going to beat your ass."

"So where is he?"

Flanagan shrugged. "That's all I heard."

On this industrial street off Westchester Square, the Rat's entrance offered the only light, a single yellow bulb that hung above a hand-painted sign, the words *Herr Fritz's Ratskeller* enclosing the face of a chubby-cheeked, white-bearded man wearing a Tyrolean hat and raising a stein of beer.

"So what do you want to do?" Johnnie Jay asked. "You want to take off?"

Hunt stared into the dark space adjacent to the building where a subway yard served as repository for old and abandoned cars as well as newer ones awaiting service. "It's my birthday," he said, heading toward the door. "It's my special night."

Inside, the room was longer than it was wide, the bar running along one wall, a dance floor at either end. All manner of

65

steins filled its nooks and crannies and the shelves above the bar, sharing that space with small carved wooden figures in Bavarian dress, legions of them, tiny armies of playful, dancing frolicking folk. Forget the Nazis, they seemed to say. Forget the horrific destruction we wreaked upon the world, let's have a beer.

Mostly the girls were B-I-C's, Bronx Irish Catholics from the local parishes. They were demure and dressed modestly, blouses and skirts, or casual summer dresses. The guys ran the gamut from Ivy League to hipsters to greasers.

And then, of course, there were the Misfits like Hunt and Johnnie Jay who considered themselves the true individualists. The downside of this, as they both knew, was that the girls at the Rat usually turned down their request for a dance. The B-I-C's were nothing if not conformist. If you didn't fit in anywhere you were a mystery, a shadow, a question mark; and these girls were not the adventurous type. They sought a transparently recognizable kind of guy.

The buzz tonight, though, up and down the bar seemed to be more about fear and danger than romance. Everyone was talking about the allegedly imminent approach of the Golden Guineas.

"... did you hear. . . ?"

"... someone said. . . ."

"... someone heard. . ."

"... someone saw. . ."

"... heading this way. . ."

"... they beat up some guys . . ."

"... big fight on Pelham Parkway, chains, bats. . . "

"... Bronx Park, too. . . "

"... bloody as hell. . ."

"... cops broke it up. . ."

"... territory . . . it's about territory . . ."

"... wanna be top dog. . ."

"... beat the shit out of the Harlem Devils. . ."

"... the Chester Kings, too. . ."

". . . hell, anybody they fight gets. . ."

". . . total control, like I said. . ."

". . . *I* heard they're looking to. . .

". . . settle some scores. . ."

". . . they try to come in here Fritz'll use one of those Lugers he's got stashed away in his office. . ."

". . . crazy motherfuckers. . ."

". . . wacko nut jobs. . ."

". . . jackass sickos. . ."

". . . bloodthirsty retards. . ."

". . . zombie creepos. . ."

One of the girls near Hunt, a stricken look on her face, turned to her friends.

"How we going to get home?"

"May we offer our services?" Johnnie Jay said, returning from the men's room. "The luxury of a six-passenger royal blue and cream two-tone Oldsmobile Rocket 88, vintage 1955."

The four girls stared at him as if he'd fallen from outer space. One of them quickly piped up. "My boyfriend will come get us."

"This car's a beaut," Johnnie Jay persisted. "V8 engine, 4 speed hydra-matic, chrome rocket airplane on the hood, more comfy a backseat than a Caddy—"

"Thanks, anyway. But no thanks."

"Consider it a standing offer," he replied. "Should said boyfriend fail to materialize."

The girls quickly shifted both their bodies and their attention, whispering and giggling among themselves.

To Hunt, Johnnie Jay said: "Plant a seed, who knows what might happen."

"Should we be keeping a scorecard?"

"No need for that, old buddy. The beating heart is our vindication." Before Hunt could ask him what he meant by that, he said: "They're heading to John's Paradise."

"Who?"

"The Golden Guineas."

"How do you know?"

"Guy in the bathroom."

"A rumble?"

"That, or for reinforcements. Bikers of the Bronx unite. Us against the world kind of thing."

But Hunt's attention had already been drawn away by some motion at the opposite end of the room. A flutter of light detached itself from the bar, moved deeper into the crowd which had grown to near capacity proportions. War Lord panic notwithstanding, the jukebox kept pumping out the hits, a tight compression of bodies bulged outward from each of the dance floors. More bodies came pouring in from the street.

He thought perhaps he had imagined the flutter of light, seeing nothing but the dull cluster of bodies, some in mid-shim-my, some standing idly around, others like a clogged stream pushing their way through the mass of flesh in hopes of reaching the bar.

She appeared then once more, the girl in the blue cotton dress, seeming to lift like a rising star above the merely mortal women around her, her luminous face, her dark hair swirling as she turned toward the exit, her beauty evident even at this distance. Then she was gone, lost in the churning mass of bodies, and he was forcing his way through the crowd at the bar like an unmoored object buffeted by a rising tide. He pushed and squeezed and shoved his way toward the door but when he reached it she was nowhere in sight.

On the street outside a taxi was depositing another round of party-goers and under the Herr Fritz sign a line of hopefuls had formed waiting to be admitted. Where could she have gone? So soon. So quickly.

He stood there, thinking she might re-appear.

What he saw instead, coming down the street from the direction of the el, were Sal and the Brandos. In full regalia now, despite the near eighty degree weather. Black leather shit-kickers on their feet, black T shirts. Motorcycle caps—not one of them owned a motorcycle—like what Brando wore in *The Wild*

Ones. Black leather jackets on the backs of which B-R-A-N-D-O was spelled out with silver studs.

Sal was in front leading the way, and beside him, holding his hand was Debby Ann, matching his forced march stride.

—15—

The sight of the Brandos was hard enough to take but seeing Debby Ann walking with them like a proud and defiant soldier in pursuit of some cause made Hunt's heart hit bottom.

He turned his back to them, began walking toward the end of the line to await re-admission, but found himself surrounded by Brandos pushing and shoving him down the alley that ran between the Rat and the subway yard.

The alley opened into the Rat's small parking area—employees only—separated from the subway yard by a chain-link fence. It was against this fence that Hunt was pushed, repeatedly, by Sal the Butcher.

There was a rhythm to the assault. Hunt could discern—even in the midst of the physical jarring to his back, his shoulders and his head—a one-two-three beat, the third beat of which was accompanied by the singing ring of the chain-links as his body was hurled against them.

It went like this: question, silence, shove:

"Why do I hate your guts?"

No reply.

Shove.

Ring-a-ling-a-ling.

"Why have I *always* hated your guts?"

No reply.

Shove.

Ring-a-ling-a-ling.

"Why am I gonna bust your face in?"

No reply.

Shove.

Ring-a-ling-a-ling.

At this point the rhythm shifted.

"What's this I'm hearing 'bout you and my girl?"

Which one, Hunt wanted to say but didn't. Debby Ann, her expression wide-eyed but otherwise vacant, stood a few feet behind Sal, next to Rudy, the squinty-eyed Brando who had watched them leaving the dance.

"What's this I'm hearing 'bout you kissin' her?"

Tried, Hunt was thinking. I only *tried* to kiss her. He looked at Debby Ann. Couldn't she come to his defense, at least on that point? But there was nothing backing up her wide-eyed stare.

Sal's face, on the other hand, told a different story. Rolling thunder in his eyes. *A hell of a lot* backing up his angry glare which was growing angrier and more hateful, moment by moment. Storm burst imminent. Hunt had raised his arms to ward off the blows that would "bust his face in" when Johnnie Jay emerged from the alley. "Hey, what's going on here?"

He was immediately surrounded by Brandos so he had to speak from the imprisoned center of a circle. "What's happening?"

"Your boy here's 'bout to get his butt whipped." Sal turned back to Hunt and shoved him again. The *ring-a-linging* sound ran down the long stretch of fence.

"You know, Sal, you're such a cliché," Johnnie Jay said. You know that, right?"

"Huh?" Sal of the stucco cheeks squared around to face this new challenge. "Who you callin' a cliché?"

71

"*You.* You're such a stereotype. That motorcycle get-up. All those zippers and chains. That faggot motorcycle cap—no wonder Brother Aloysius calls you *Sallie*. The way you stomp around in those boots. You think you're some kind of rebel, some kind of hero, but you're just like a thousand other bikers—except of course you don't have a bike."

Johnnie Jay paused to accentuate that particular fact. "You're common, is what I'm saying. Even your gang's name is derivative, totally unoriginal. I mean, come on. The *Brandos?* Naming it after some faggot actor in a dumb Hollywood movie? How pathetic can you get? You're a dime a dozen, common as dirt, indistinguishable from the crowd."

Johnnie Jay took a breath, drew his shoulders back. "So here's what I'm suggesting. Why don't you break the mold? For once in your life, become your own man. Why settle for being a pale shadow of the Golden Guineas or the Viceroys or the Red Wings or the Egyptian Kings or the Jesters or the Deuces or any other gang you want to name when you can be so much more? Why settle for being a *stereotype* when you can be an *archetype*?"

"An arc-a-what?" Sal had trouble getting the word out. "What the hell you talkin' about?"

"Break the mold, man. Instead of being the same old run-of-the-mill, stomp-on- your-face tough ass, instead of bopping, japping, burning, busting or mixing, instead of the same old tired rumble, show off your better side. Show some love and kindness—"

"What kind of faggot bullshit—?"

Before Sal could turn the full pressure of his rage on Johnnie Jay, there was a commotion on the street. It had begun moments before as a low rumble in the distance, exploding now in the revs and stuttering pops and chugs of a line of choppers parading toward the entrance to the Rat.

"Golden Guineas!" one of the Brandos shouted and all of them, Sal leading the way, leapt onto the fence and began climbing.

One by one they straddled the prongs at the top of the fence, Sal the most awkward of them all, gingerly trying not to rip his jeans or his jacket, finally losing his balance and, with arms flailing, falling hard on his knees on the far side. Groaning and muttering, he pulled himself to his feet and joined the other Brandos in retreat, their flickering shadows melting into the darker and larger shadows of the stalled subway cars.

The only people left in the parking area were Hunt, Johnnie Jay, and Debby Ann whose wide-eyed stare was now filled with disbelief. Before Hunt could offer her a ride home, she turned on her heel and marched toward the street.

Apparently the Golden Guineas had come by simply to make a statement because after circling in the street for several minutes they moved on, single file again, weaving their way toward the el and beyond.

In the sudden silence, Hunt realized how profusely he'd been sweating. He wiped his face and neck with a handkerchief and looked to Johnnie Jay who was staring into the subway yard where all trace of the Brandos had been erased.

Hunt said, "Your Low-ness owes your High-ness a debt of gratitude."

"No problem, man. A case of knowledge triumphing over ignorance."

"A case of fate being on our side."

"That, too."

"Hey, by the way, how'd you know all that gang slang?"

Johnnie Jay laughed. "What do you think I do when I'm supposed to be studying? I read up on things, man. Like gang culture. Beats those math problems I can't figure out."

Inside the Rat the music had started up again, thumping through the cinder block wall that lined the alley. Johnnie Jay stared at the wall as if the music might transform it, re-configure it into the shapes of the girls dancing inside. "You want to go back in? Debby Ann might be there."

Hunt considered. "What would be the point?"

"So where do you want to go?"

73

"John's Paradise."

"You crazy? That's where the Golden Guineas are headed."

"Precisely."

Johnnie Jay shook his head. "Make sense, man."

"You're the one who's always saying we should open ourselves to experience, right?"

"You say it, too."

"Exactly. And what better place to be, experience-wise, on this particular night that used to be my birthday than with the Golden Guineas on what might be one of the most significant moments in recent Bronx history?" If you can't have love, Hunt was thinking, then experience—in whatever raw, disheveled and disorganized way it presented itself to you—would have to do.

He had turned back to the subway yard where in a far corner he saw a figure moving between cars. At first, he thought it must be one of the Brandos but the figure moved too slowly, was hunched over and stumbling, and he decided it had to be one of the old, homeless men rumored to live in the yard. He watched the man slowly cross the open space between cars until he became indistinguishable from the shadows.

Johnnie Jay joined him at the fence. "So what do you think? Sal's going out with Debby Ann now. That mean I have a shot at Angelina?"

—16—

At John's Paradise, Hunt cautioned Johnnie Jay to park a block away. Should there be trouble in the form of fights or gang warfare, the Rocket 88 would be spared damage. As they walked toward the entrance, the cemetery where Toby was buried stretched away on the far side of the street, a quiet land of darkness in contrast to the hammering noise of the music that spilled from the bar.

For a moment, glancing at the cemetery wall and the line of trees that hid the long rows of tombstones, he saw *Toby running toward him with his blonde curls jiggling, his crooked giddy grin, his eyes overflowing with delight, arms spread wide. Inside himself Hunt was shouting, "Stop! Stop!" When Toby reached the street, he did stop running, standing still at the curb, frozen there in time and memory, waiting;* and the hard pounding of Hunt's heart slowly returned to normal again and his breath came easier, steady once more.

"What's the matter?" Johnnie Jay asked.

Hunt turned away from the cemetery and forced a smile. "Nothing. Nothing."

The street ahead was lined with a precise row of bikes,

chrome glinting under the street lights, though none bore the Golden Guineas' insignia: a rod with a spiked metal ball at its tip, a capital *G* on either side.

Usually Hunt came here alone, when Johnnie Jay was otherwise engaged. He liked it because it made him feel close to Toby and he liked the anonymity that allowed him to sit in a corner of the bar, drink a beer, and watch the girls dance.

The girls at John's Paradise wore the tightest pants in the borough. Their T-shirts and halter tops were tight, too. Even the way they danced was tight: small circles of taut steps, hips twitching, arms close at their sides.

As they entered, the music cut off, the sudden silence a shock. The band members were setting down their guitars.

The place smelled of armpits.

Hunt led the way to the bar, threading gingerly between thick tattooed arms, leather vests, black-booted feet. You didn't want to bump anyone. You didn't want to piss anyone off.

The bartender, Artie, asked him how they were hanging.

"They're hanging good," Hunt said. "Hanging real good." Never show your pain. Not in a place like this. "Two Rolling Rocks."

Artie was a squat, tank of a guy with arms the size of thighs. Hard face, kind smile. He was a biker himself until two bad spills, the consequences of which could be seen in the halting, stiff-legged way he walked, had removed him from the scene. For some reason he'd taken a liking to Hunt. Never once had he asked him for I.D. Nor did he ask now to see Johnnie Jay's. He was as contemptuous of the law as were the clientele.

Over time, he'd mentored Hunt on how to survive a night of drinking at the Paradise. Which girls not to dance with. Not her or her or her. Don't even think about asking *that* one.

On the dance floor, Artie had cautioned, do nothing excessive. Keep your hands and arms close. Don't call attention to yourself.

Not that Hunt thought too seriously about dancing with anyone. The women seemed too street-smart, too tough, too indifferent. Even the ones his own age seemed too old for him. But he appreciated the advice, anyway.

And then Artie's more general advice. No eye contact with any of the guys. Use the men's room only when it's unoccupied. Don't hog the pinball machines, the phone, the jukebox or too much bar space. And never, never touch anyone's bike out on the street.

Other than that, man, enjoy the hell outta the place, Artie would say and laugh his way back to the other end of the bar.

When he brought the Rolling Rocks, Hunt asked him if the Golden Guineas had shown up.

"Who wants to know?" he said it dead-serious, as if the information were classified.

"Just curious."

"Don't be." He paused to let Hunt think about that. "They might want to know who's checking up on them. You don't want to be a name on their list." Then he laughed and leaned across the bar, lowering his voice, an example to Hunt to keep his own voice down.

"Been here and gone. Real quick stop. Wham, Bam, thank you, ma'am." Artie chuckled. "Seems they've got some scores to settle. Local gangs on their shit list. Came in for directions, so to speak."

"From who?"

Artie gave him a disapproving scowl.

"Sorry."

Folks in here want you to know something, Artie had once advised him, they'll tell you. They don't offer it, don't ask. "Sorry," Hunt said again.

"No problem, kid." He leaned with mock-confidentiality toward Hunt. "There is something I *can* tell you, though."

"What's that?"

"The latest rumor."

"Yeah?"

"From reliable sources."

"Tell me."

"Bobby Darin might make a surprise appearance tonight?"

"Where?"

"McMann's."

"You're kidding, right? That's where we're heading."

"That's the word," Artie said.

Johnnie Jay began babbling about how there wasn't any-body in the Bronx didn't look up to Darin. Local hero. Ordinary guy from the most ordinary of places who was making it big.

"Know what his real name is?" Artie asked.

Hunt shook his head no.

"Walden Cassotto. Don't sound as good, but he never should've changed it. A person should be who he is." He was wiping down the bar. "Wish I could get out of here for a few hours. Might be the last time we get to see him playing local, what with him going off to Hollywood. He won't be one of us anymore."

The jukebox was silent but on the dance floor a biker girl danced by herself in slow, uneven circles. She was drunk or stoned, her eyes half-closed, her narrow face clenched tight in concentration as if the song she was remembering came from long ago and far away.

Before heading up to McMann's, Hunt wanted to visit To-by's grave.

"Dark as hell in there, man," Johnnie Jay said.

"It's light enough." He'd been there before at night, usually on nights like this, after a few beers at the Paradise.

The lock on the gate was broken, so it was easy to slip in. Once inside, it was like the world had disappeared. At least that was the way it was for Hunt. The street was lost behind a row of trees. Occasionally there was the sound of a car horn or an en-gine backfiring, but those sounds receded as they moved deeper into the cemetery until finally even the music from the bar be-came indistinct. The piping chatter of crickets replaced it, and a stillness that made the far-off hum of traffic heading for the

78

Whitestone Bridge sound like wind.

The rows of tombstones were long and seemingly endless, luminous in the moon's faint light.

"Creepy in here," Johnnie Jay said.

"Can't you feel him—his spirit?"

It—his spirit—grew stronger the closer they came to his grave. Not only Hunt felt that way. Johnnie Jay, walking a few feet behind Hunt, thought he could feel it, too. "Like something taking your hand," was the way he described it.

A few minutes later, though, doubt again invaded Johnnie Jay's voice. "How do you find your way? Everything looks the same."

"Not everything."

Hunt had his markers: a tree; an unusually ornate angel rising from a headstone; his instinct. "Some things you just know how to find."

Toby's grave was in the middle of one of the longest rows. The stone was plain, almost flat on the earth. To Hunt's way of thinking, it was too plain. It seemed lost in the long line of markers. Too easy to overlook, too indistinguishable from the graves around it for a kid who was so special, so spilling over with life.

Standing there, staring at the stone, he saw Toby's irresistible grin. He recited to himself, as he always did on these visits, the prayer he'd composed long ago.

Toby, don't be scared. Toby, be brave.

Toby, don't be lonely. Toby, be strong.

Now he added: *I'm walking with you. Wherever you go, I'm holding your hand.*

And that brought the memory back unbroken.

Toby riding his tricycle on the Oval's walkway.

Toby seeing him on the far side of the street.

Toby running through the flower beds, through the hedges.

Toby running across the grass. Toby on the sidewalk.

His own voice yelling, "Stop. Stop."

Toby at the curb, not hearing, not listening, not stopping.

Wide crooked grin, arms spread wide.

The white van.

Brakes grinding.

Too late. Too late.

"My fault," he said aloud now to Toby, to the flat white stone.

"You know that's not true," Johnnie Jay said.

"It *feels* true."

"It was an accident. Everybody knows that. Everybody said that. Nobody blames you."

"Except me."

"Come on, guy, don't do this."

"If I hadn't waved to him. If he hadn't seen me—" He'd traveled this ground so many times. A continuous, never-ending journey that took place on a distant horizon beyond whatever else was happening to him at the moment. At times, like right this minute, it felt as if he were living two lives simultaneously.

"You ever think that maybe this was pre-ordained?" Johnnie Jay said.

"Pre-destination, you mean?"

"Maybe it's part of the plan. Each of us is given our own special pain to carry. Like a burden. Like a test. The Sisyphus thing."

"Why, though?"

"The wrong question, my man. It's *how*, not *why*." He thought a moment, staring off at the dark line of trees along the cemetery wall. "And look at it this way. It's not something you have to run away from. You got this beautiful four year-old kid to carry around inside you. You bring him back to life each time you think of him."

—17—

On the drive to McMann's Johnnie Jay sang along to the radio with his wavering, slightly off-key baritone. He kept glancing over at Hunt who was turned away, staring at the empty lots of Castle Hill but seeing Toby playing in the grass of the Oval, those moments before he ran toward the street.

Johnnie Jay said, "Come on, man, I need some help here. Don't leave me twisting in the wind. I need some *harmony.*" He sang more of the song, solo, and finally, on the last chorus, Hunt joined in with a plaintive, self-mocking whine: "*why must I be. . . ?*" The misery to supersede all miseries: teenage romance. The question without an answer: why must I be a teenager in love?

From that point on, with the volume knob on the radio turned down, they concocted a song of their own with a medley of phrases from the top forty, staying true to the mournful frustrations of teenage heartbreak: . . .*no one knows. . .my tears are falling. . .pity my heart. . .I'm a fool to care. . .with all my heart and soul . . . darling, please please come back . . .everything reminds me of. . .you. . .you . . . you . . . you . . . YOUUUUU!*

"I guess it's true," Johnnie Jay said when they'd run out of words. "All the best tunes say so."

"What's true?"

"The heart is a lonely hunter. No pun intended."

Hunt was thinking long-term. "You think we'll be like this at fifty?"

"Like what?"

"Riding around like this. Bar to bar. Feeling low."

"Jeez, I hope not."

"What if we are?"

"I don't know. We'll figure it out then, I guess. But more than likely we'll have ten kids and a grumpy wife and we won't have time to figure anything out."

Hunt stared across an empty lot at the end of which several apartment buildings were under development. There were plans to make the entire avenue one big city housing project. "I saw her tonight."

"Who?"

"*Her.*"

"Who's *her*?"

"This dream girl."

"Who is she?"

"She's beautiful. Truly, truly beautiful."

"Where'd you see her?"

"At the dance. At the Rat, too."

"You know her name?"

"No."

"She from the neighborhood?"

"I don't know."

"So?" Johnnie Jay glanced at him, waiting for more. "What?"

"What *what*?"

"What's she like? Real beautiful, you say?"

"It's more than that."

Johnnie Jay was wide-eyed. "Yeah?"

"It was like she was *it*."

"It?"

"The end. The finish line. Like there was nothing more.

There was nowhere else to go."

"Wow!"

"Yeah."

"So what's the plan?"

"No plan."

"You've *got* to have a plan."

"I know. I know."

"So what's the plan?"

"I'm working on it."

"You have to talk to her, man. You have to find out who she is."

"Maybe she's not even real. Maybe I made her up."

"Of course, she's real. You saw her, didn't you? *Couple* of times, right?"

"Yeah."

"So she's real."

"Maybe."

"We've got to find her." Johnnie Jay pounded the steering wheel with excitement. "A quest. We're on a quest. She's going to be at McMann's. I know it. *Every*body's going to be at McMann's." He thought some more about it. "What if she's not from the neighborhood? What if she's only visiting, passing through? Tonight might be your only chance. Oh my god."

"Oh my god, what?"

"Imagine the sorrow. Your dream appears and is gone. You spend your whole life knowing you were *this* close." He raised his hand, thumb and forefinger almost touching. "*This* close."

Johnnie Jay slammed his open palm against the wheel. "Damn, we can't let that happen. We can't. We just can't. We can't let you fall victim to a lifetime of remorse."

Ahead, the traffic had grown heavy and he was forced to slow down. "Look at this. We're still three blocks away. The lot's going to be full."

"There," Hunt said. "Park there," and Johnnie Jay swung the car abruptly to the right and slipped in between two Impalas parked against the wire netting of a golf driving range.

83

On the solid part of the fence below the netting, someone had scrawled: *the truest hole in one is the hole in your heart.*

They walked along the fence toward the avenue which dead-ended against the Long Island Sound. This part of Castle Hill was like a faded beach town. Miniature golf, a baseball batting range, and the now-defunct Castle Hill Beach and Tennis club, which had been a fancy name for a rather cheesy—to Hunt's mind—run-down, low-rent resort. This was what they had instead of Coney Island.

He'd spent the summer of his freshman year working here, cleaning the pool—there was no actual beach—and supplying towels to the bratty kids and sullen moms who spent their time lounging on the rickety, falling apart deck chairs and complaining how hot it was or how bad was the smell of the mudflats that came drifting over the pink and white bath house.

The beach club was directly across the street from Mc-Mann's—the bar's full name was McMann's-by-the-Sea—and as they walked into the parking lot they caught a whiff themselves of the mudflats, bringing with it a host of insipid memories Hunt would as soon not be reminded of.

Lines of people streamed between the parked cars on the way to the entrance of the squat two-story wood frame building at the far end.

They had made it halfway there when Hunt heard Lee Andrews singing *Try the Impossible.* The song gave him pause, brought Debby Ann center stage again in his mind, dancing close to her—or as close as she would let him—and for reasons he wasn't sure of he found himself drifting in the direction of the car on whose radio it was playing. He passed Fairlanes, Bonnevilles, Catalina's, Plymouth Fury's, chopped and blocked Mercs, and an occasional exotic like a T-Bird or a Vette.

"Come on. Let's go in. We don't want to miss anything," Johnnie Jay called behind him, having recognized the car and its occupants before Hunt did. "Come *onnnn.*"

His warning came too late. It was Sal's gold Caddy—really Sal's father's car—and at the same time Hunt identified it, he saw the shadows on the front seat. The shadows divided then, the section nearest him turned and he saw Sal's slicked back hair, the head it belonged to bent forward kissing Debby Ann.

Hunt, head bowed, whirled on his heel and came running back down the row as if he might outdistance the hurt.

Johnnie Jay clamped his arm around him, pulled him toward the entrance. "She's ancient history now. Let's go find the dream girl."

—18—

Johnnie Jay led the search. They began at the large, rectangular bar in the room's center, working their way in the dim blue light, a slow thread-like weaving through the crowd. Large groups, small groups, couples, loners. A human telephone line passing messages about the possible appearance of the borough's brightest star. For the time being, the threat of the Golden Guineas no longer dominated the chatter.

It took them nearly fifteen minutes to circle the bar once.

No sighting of the dream girl.

"Tell me again what she looks like," Johnnie Jay said.

"Dark hair. Thin, long legs. Really nice face."

"You can't be more specific?"

"Like I said it's her face that's extraordinary. Kind of ethereal, you know. But earthy, too. Like she's connected to the moon *and* the earth."

Johnnie Jay raised his eyebrows. "That really helps a lot."

They went around a second time, as if she'd been hiding and might surface at any moment and separate herself from the hundreds of other faces hovering before them.

After that, they cruised the dance floor but she wasn't

among the dancers. Hunt stared through the long row of windows that faced out onto a flagstone-lined deck beyond which the Sound was visible, dark and heaving beneath the sliver moon's light. It didn't appear she was on the deck, either, but Johnnie Jay insisted they search through the smaller crowd that had gathered there, some standing, some seated at umbrella-topped tables, each holding a drink in hand like a ticket to their expectations.

Back inside they watched the band struggle through an anemic version of *Suzie-Q*.

"Maybe she's been here and left," Johnnie Jay said. Quickly, to keep hope alive, he added: "Or maybe she hasn't gotten here yet."

"Hey, guys," a voice behind them said. Norm Blevsky, dressed in a bright red Hawaiian shirt hanging over his yellow Bermuda shorts. The shirt featured dozens of gold fish swimming vertically rather than horizontally, their mouths gaping and contorted, so that it appeared they were drowning in a sea of blood.

"Guess what?" he said now.

Hunt and Johnnie Jay stared at him blankly, saying nothing.

"Numbers 91, 92 and 93 so far tonight. Here goes 94." He walked over to a red-haired girl wearing a St. Helena T-shirt. She promptly turned him down with a shake of her head. Blevsky thanked her, bowed from the waist and walked away with his head held high as if he'd been awarded a medal.

He jumped onto the stage and began a herky-jerky, exaggerated solo dance alongside the drummer who cast a continuing belligerent glare his way. In a matter of moments, two bouncers dragged Blevsky from the stage and hustled him out the side door onto the deck.

"Weirdest cat alive," Johnnie Jay said.

"But a true individual, nonetheless."

Johnnie Jay looked at him askance. "How you figure that?"

"He is who he is. He doesn't hide it."

87

"Maybe he should."

But as much as Hunt wanted to join in the near-unanimous ridicule of the guy, he had to give him credit, too. He lived out on the edge somewhere, true to his own weirdness, and that took courage, more than any ordinary person had, more—to be sure—than his ridiculing classmates had. He was a loner of extraordinary proportions.

"He's an artist of sorts, if you think about it."

"I'd rather not think about it," Johnnie Jay said and laughed. "Hey, there's your ardent admirer and devotee." He was waving at Caroline Longo who emerged from the crowd and came over with her best friend, Annie Rizzo.

"Hey, guys," Caroline said. "We've been looking for somebody to dance with."

Lame as they thought the band was, they were out on the floor swinging with the rest of the crowd, Annie dancing with Johnnie Jay, Caroline with Hunt.

She was her usual brown-eyed, rosy cheeked high-spirited self. "You remember those new steps?"

" 'Course I do." And to prove it Hunt led her through the steps she'd taught him, adding a few extra twists and spins of his own. Her enthusiasm was contagious and they danced six straight songs without taking a break. For that time he was able to forget about Debby Ann and Sal in the car. It was only the music, the big beat, and swinging arms and legs.

But when they stopped finally, sweating and breathless, the memory came back like a weight pulling him underwater. He struggled to stay above the surface. "So what do you hear about Bobby Darin?"

"Somebody said he was on his way. And somebody else said he'd been outside in the parking lot when he heard the Golden Guineas were coming and he turned around and went home."

"Is that true?"

"Is what true?"

"The Guineas are coming."

She shrugged. "It's all rumors. You can pick whichever one you want to believe."

"I guess it makes sense."

"What does?"

"That he wouldn't want to be here if there's trouble."

She nodded at the dance floor and the throngs clustered around the bar. "Lots of us are willing to take that chance, though, aren't we?" In the band's momentary pause between songs, her laugh hung in the air, nowhere to go. She looked at Hunt but his mind had drifted off.

It was the smoky blue light in the room and the moody ballad the band slipped into that brought Debby Ann back to life again, an aching sore that wouldn't heal. He looked over at Johnnie Jay who was dancing close with Annie Rizzo, a dreamy self-satisfied look on his face.

That was the difference between them, Hunt thought. The *big* difference.

His friend could get lost in the moment for long periods of time; contentment blessed him with all its benevolence. And though Hunt could be distracted briefly, here and there, contentment and its riches eluded him.

There was always something missing.

Something right beyond his reach.

—19—

Sal and Debby Ann had finally come in from the parking lot.

Not only were her bangs twisted and damp against her skin, her entire head of hair had fallen, hanging flat and straight and without shine. Something else wasn't right about her face—her eyes, bleary and dazed. She looked as if she'd been rained on.

From the bar where he nursed a beer, Hunt watched them slow dance. Debby seemed to melt into Sal, a complete submission that included her draping both her arms around his neck, hanging onto him in a way that made it impossible for him to move independently of her, or her of him. In the shadowed light, they stood almost motionless: one person, one desire. Painful as it was, he couldn't take his eyes from them.

Until Sal saw him watching. He jerked back abruptly, freeing himself from Debby Ann and lurching toward Hunt until she slipped her hand around his waist, let it linger there open-palmed an inch or two below his belt buckle. She slid back in front of him and tilted her head to be kissed.

Sal obliged, and the crisis passed.

At least for the moment.

Hunt could still feel the violence in the greaser's eyes, the fury in the taut muscles of his face. He thought it best to move around to the far side of the bar where his view of the dance floor was less direct.

He was alone at the moment, Caroline and Annie having gone home to meet their two a.m. curfew, Johnnie Jay trolling the darker corners of the room in hopes of finding an overlooked gem—someone shy but willing, was the way he described this woman of his fantasy.

The crowd had thinned somewhat, three deep at the bar instead of six. Hope for a Bobby Darin appearance, however, had not diminished.

"They come in late," someone nearby was saying. "That's the way these stars like to do it. They turn up when you least expect it."

Johnnie Jay showed up then, weary-eyed and disappointed, looking the worse for his search.

"No luck?"

"Nada." He looked disconsolately up and down the bar. "You know that saying about how the girls get better looking at closing time? I don't think that's true. They get sadder looking, is what they get."

He ordered a beer, for the road. "You ready to go?"

"I'm going to stick around," Hunt said.

"Yeah?"

"Yeah." And because Johnnie Jay seemed to be waiting for an explanation of some kind, he added: "I feel like it's still my birthday. I feel like the night's not over yet."

"Yeah?"

"Something's going to happen. I want to be around when it does."

"Told my father I'd have the car back by three. Otherwise, I'd stay." He checked the clock above the bar. "How you gonna get home?"

"The bus is still running."

"Oh, yeah, right." He drank down his beer and belched.

91

He looked toward the door but didn't move. "I should go."

"Yeah."

"Maybe the dream girl will still show."

"Maybe."

"If she does, don't let her get away." He glanced toward the door again but kept his hands curled tight around the rim of the bar. "I should go. You okay?"

"I'll be okay."

"I'll come back, if it's not too late. I'll drop the keys off, wait till my old man gets back to sleep." He leaned away from the bar. "See ya."

"See ya."

He had taken a few steps toward the door when he stopped and turned. "If Angelina Lanzalotto shows up, give her a message for me, will you?"

"Sure, what?"

"Tell her," he groped for the right words. "Tell her—" He made one more effort before conceding defeat. "I don't know," he said. "Tell her to wait for me."

He laughed and made his way finally out the door.

—20—

The Blue Mood was threatening when Hunt happened to turn toward the row of windows that overlooked the deck and saw the dream girl again.

One moment it was an ordinary view of outdoor tables, anonymous faces and dark sky; the next, there she was: an apparition, a mirage.

She was alone, crossing the deck, not quickly but with purpose as if she'd drifted in from the mystical waters of the Sound on a mission of some kind, her dark hair loose and flowing, her blue dress gossamer-thin and lifted by the breeze.

Again he felt his breath catch, his heartbeat jumping tracks, ticking down his bones, in every muscle and tendon.

He hurried to the side door, flinging it open, feeling the clarifying weight of the salt-tinged air that for the moment was unsullied by the odor of the mud flats. He had no idea what he would say to her. *Some*thing. He stared down the length of the deck but couldn't see her.

Two girls in tight jeans and short-sleeved knit tops and nearly identical beehive hair-do's sat at a nearby table. He started to ask, "Did you see—?" but hurried past them without finishing.

He wove his way between the few lingering outdoor drinkers until he reached the steps to the parking lot, less than a third filled now. Walking between what was left of the rows, he peered into each of the remaining cars, annoying more than a few couples in the midst of their mad make-out sessions.

"Hey, beat it, scumbag. . . ."

"Up yours, you peeping Tom asshole. . . ."

"Hey, I know that guy. He's the douche bag at the beach. . . ."

"What kinda perv are you, anyway. . .?"

Slouching away, he expected at any moment the angry weight of a beer can landing against his shoulders or the back of his head.

As he mounted the steps to the deck, he wondered where she could have gone. Would she have wandered out to the rocky shoreline? He didn't think so. There was no path here that would have made the water accessible.

He stood on the deck uncertainly. It was empty now save for the two girls with the beehives. They had moved to a table closer to the railing and they were staring dully, in silence, across the water at the lights of the bridge.

"You didn't happen to see someone, did you?" he asked, approaching them.

"Who?"

They were both petite with thin narrow faces, so similarly dressed they might have been twins, except that one had dark hair and the other was blonde. It was the blonde who had responded.

It was the blonde who said now, "Hey, you want to buy me and Junie a drink?"

Hunt stopped and looked from one to the other. They each bore a similar washed-out, jaded expression.

"I'm Lorie," the blonde said. "And this here's Junie."

The best Hunt could muster at the moment was a weak, "Hello."

"So whaddya think?" Lorie sat with her back arched, her

face tilted toward him, as if she were posing for something. "You wanna buy us a drink?"

"Sure, I guess." He couldn't think of a good reason not to, except for the money he'd be spending, and they looked like they needed cheering up. "What are you drinking?"

"Gin and tonic for me, Vodka Collins for her."

"Make mine a double," Junie said. "They're real stingy here with their shots."

Hunt took their glasses and went inside.

It was almost three and most of the crowd had left. Sal and Debby Ann were long gone. A lone couple occupied the dance floor, kissing as they stood there, hardly moving to the slowest, grittiest version of *Harlem Nocturne* Hunt had ever heard.

The sound the sax player coaxed from his instrument came from some deep and forbidden place, the blue and plaintive notes intensified by the room's now empty reaches—the long hollowed-out echo of a soul's longing.

Or so it seemed to Hunt.

—21—

When he brought the drinks outside, Lorie sat alone at the table.

"Where's Junie?"

"Ladies room."

He set the two glasses down.

"Where's yours?" she wanted to know.

What he didn't say was that he'd already spent more than half of his week's salary and that even if he'd wanted another beer he wouldn't dare use any more of the money he was supposed to be saving. "I've had enough for one night."

"Not *me*. Not after the night me and Junie just had." She sipped steadily from the straw, finishing more than half her drink.

"You two are sisters?"

"Everybody thinks so," she said, finding that amusing. "Everybody thinks we look alike, talk alike, dress alike. And the truth of the matter is, we *could* be sisters. We've known each other forever." She continued sipping her drink until only ice cubes remained in her glass, then she reached for Junie's. "But we're real different. *Inside.* I'm the stable one, you could say. She's kinda out on the edge sometimes. Know what I mean?"

"Sort of, I guess."

She sucked on the straw of the Vodka Collins and said, "I'm real thirsty, you know," before pushing it away as an act of self-control.

"It's not that I don't love her, I do. I really do. She's the best of the best. But she's always doing something crazy. Junie, I mean. Like tonight, for example. She wants to go to this party over at 149ᵗʰ and Melrose. Some guy she met. Great guy, she says. And all of his friends are gonna be there. All great guys, according to him. She's sure there's gonna be someone just right for me. Gonna be a lot of laughs, she says. Backyard barbeque and all that. Tons of beer and booze, good music, dancing, the whole nine yards.

"Well, I don't know if you know it but it's not such a great neighborhood over there. Pretty wild, from what I hear. Lot of down guys. Lot of heads get busted. So I'm not real keen on this party idea, but she keeps nagging me on. Says we always do what *I* want to do, never what *she* wants to do—which by the way is not at all true, and I tell her that. I tell her right to her face, it's not true. Not that she listens. Not that she pays me any mind. Not her. Not Junie. When she gets an idea into her head, the blinders come on. Can't see left or right, top or bottom, just straight ahead, just straight to where she wants to go.

"So I give in. Against my better judgment. I give in 'cause she wears me down to the point I can't take it anymore. I give in just to shut her up. I even offer to take *my* car. Now why did I do that?"

Hunt thought she expected an answer but she rushed on before he could offer one.

"Why? I ask myself, why, why, why? And you *know* why? Because I'm a good person, that's why. That's the plain and simple fact of it. I don't like friction. I don't like when things get all tense. I don't like the way she's gonna be pissed off at me all night if we don't go. See what I mean?"

"I do," Hunt said, knowing that was the response she wanted.

97

"So we take my car. Full tank of gas and all, so I don't even have to ask her to chip in, not a penny. All she has to do is sit there like the princess she thinks she is while I chauffeur her around, up this street, down that one, getting lost three times before we get there and like I said, like I knew it would be, the street gives me the creeps, all these dudes hangin' out in dark doorways and store fronts. I say maybe we should go back home, find something else to do but she starts in again, nag, nag, nag. So we find the house and go in.

"*Nothin'* like she said it would be. Oh, there were guys all right, all kinds of guys, not another chick in sight, though. No music, like she said. No barbeque, no dancing. Guys running all over the place, putting together a stockpile. 'What happened to the party?' she asks the guy who invited her. 'Change a plans,' he says. 'Somethin' heavy's going down.' 'What?' she asks. 'What's going down?' And he tells her, 'the GG's are comin'. They're getting ready to burn.'"

"The GG's?" Hunt asked. "You mean the Golden Guineas?"

"I can't say their name."

"Why not?"

"It's this thing I have. I say their name out loud, I'll be punished. They'll get me. They're pretty heavy dudes."

"Some people feel that way about saying God's name."

"Oh, yeah?" She looked at him blankly, not seeing the connection. "So anyway what these guys are doing is getting ready to rumble. They're stockpiling their weapons. Broom handles, bike chains, garrison belts, bats, switchblades, car aerials, belts with metal buckles, zip guns, you name it. They're making this pile in the basement like it's the Alamo or something.

"So I grab Junie's hand and yank her out of there. For once, she doesn't resist. For once, she just shuts her mouth and gets in the car. So I'm drivin' on 149th, not speeding or nothing, just drivin' nice as you please and I don't make it halfway across and I get pulled over by the cops. Comes outta nowhere, siren screaming, lights flashing so bright I nearly hit another

98

car trying to pull to the curb. Says I ran a light but I know for a fact that ain't true cause the light was still yellow when I went through, I swear to God and that's what I said to him, that I'd swear on a stack of Bibles but he says he got me dead to rights, won't listen to my side of it at all, and writes me up. And you know the worst part of it?"

"No," Hunt said.

"Worst part of it is I know the guy. Met him one night in a bar in Morris Park. Wouldn't go home with him like he wanted. So that's what this whole thing was about. Not a thing to do with the law."

Hunt had never heard someone talk so fast about so little. He was trying to figure whether it was worse for a woman to talk too much, like Lorie, or too little like Debby Ann. At least with Lorie, he concluded, you had *some* idea of what was going on inside her.

She reached over and sipped again, greedily, from Junie's Vodka Collins. "So we stop for a drink at Murphy's on East Tremont—try to recoup, ya know—and when we come outside someone's bent my aerial and keyed both doors, and I'm thinkin' can this night get any worse? You know the only thing I could think of that would cheer me up?"

Hunt had no idea.

"A White Castle."

She licked her lips and broke into a smile. "One of my favorite things in this whole dismal world, no doubt about it. So we stopped at the one on Bruckner, ya know, across from the used car lot. I love everything about those burgers, ya know? The bun, those tiny pieces of chopped-up onions, that skinny slice of pickle, the little square shape of them. Ya know? That square shape is what makes them what they are. It affects the taste. I don't know how, but it does. I'm sure of it. Unique. Truly unique. The way the patty and the bun kinda melt together, all soft and mushy. Whoever dreamed that up's got to be a real genius. Don't you think?"

"Probably."

"Marry him in a minute, he asked me. I would, too," she said, thinking Hunt was doubting her. "Spend my whole life in the kitchen, watching him cook."

What Hunt was in fact thinking was that she seemed so agitated he should ask her to dance. Maybe that would calm her down, make her feel better.

So he did.

She bumped the table when she stood but then steadied herself, waiting for him. When he reached for her, she slid without hesitation into his arms, pressing herself so tight against him he could feel the heat where their bodies joined below the waist. The rest of her, too, fit so snugly in his arms he was reminded of a small animal burrowing into its hole for warmth.

The slow music from the band bled through the walls and for several seconds they swayed against each other. He rested his hand on her neck, gently touching her tower of hair, stiff and straw-like against his fingers.

"Careful," she said and he moved his hand so it wasn't touching her hair.

"Junie," he said. "She's been gone a while. You think she's all right?"

"She can take of herself," Lorie said. "That girl could spend the whole night in the ladies room. Her and her can of Aqua-Net. She whirls that thing around her head like she was roping a calf then waits for the mist to fall like it was rain on parched earth."

She drew her head back then, her face relaxed, almost serene, as she studied *his* face closely before asking how old he was. Her breath smelled of onions.

Hunt figured she had to be at least twenty-two, maybe twenty-three so to be safe he said, "Twenty-four."

"Oh."

He tried to read her tone and her expression for surprise or doubt. At the same time she continued to scrutinize him in a verification process of her own.

"O god," she said at last: a long slow sigh. "O god. O god. O god."

"O god, what?"

"Everything. And nothing." Her sour breath rose in the close air between them.

He liked the feel of her body, especially the way she made him feel between his legs, but he turned his head slightly to avoid the direct onslaught of her breath.

"This place," she said. "This McMann's-by-the-Sea. Kind of a disappointment, ya know. I mean, when you hear about it, it sounds fabulous. Live music, big crowds, outdoor deck, view of the bridge, the lights of ships passing by. But when you're here, no big deal. It's just some ordinary place: skimpy drinks, so-so band, and this—this deck. I mean, it overlooks the water but you can't get *to* it, the water. All these weeds and rocks and mud. What the hell kind of crummy beach is that? And the smell. Like every living thing in the Sound up and kicked the bucket at the same time."

Her face had lost its momentary serenity. Once again, it looked pinched and narrow, her eyes darting here and there, her pupils on the run in the trapped space of her sockets.

He knew what she meant. It was the Conspiracy of the Recalcitrant Circumstance. The way it worked, and it always worked the exact same way, was this: there were all these circumstances that contributed to making a moment—an event or experience—wonderful. But there was always at least one circumstance in the set of circumstances that wasn't right, that kept the moment from being perfect.

Like right now, dancing close with Lorie, it was a White Castle hamburger eaten hours earlier that left its stain on the night air, turned his head away, kept their lips from touching.

The music had stopped. Through the windows he could see the band packing up their instruments, but Lorie still clung to him and he held her, his face averted, as if nothing had changed. Far off, on the water, a ship horn sounded and mo-

101

ments later another boat returned its call.

"Hey," she said at last, stepping back then, looking concerned. "Maybe I *should* go check on Junie. Wait here for me, okay?"

"Okay."

She searched his face, determining if he could be trusted. "You'll be here, won't you?"

"Yes."

"You're sure?"

"Yes."

"I wanna see she's okay, that's all." She reached across the table for the now less-than-half full Vodka Collins. "I'll bring her this." She offered Hunt her tight, pinched smile. "Be right back, honey. Okay?"

"Okay."

No one, except his Aunt Josie, had ever called him *honey* before.

While he sat waiting for her, the Blue Mood finally over-took him.

It made him feel strangely alone, disconnected: from this deck, this table where he was sitting, from the dark waters of the Sound which now seemed darker and without end, from the lights of the bridge which had lost their color, shining now coldly white and thin as ice. It felt as if there was no place in this world for him, no other being to share it with; there was no past or future, not even the present moment to hold, no hope of love or kindness or mercy.

A weakness spread through him, a trembling of muscle and bone, as if he were the lone witness of his own vanishing act. Only his eyes remained and what they saw offered him no comfort. They showed him this empty deck, the night failing all around him. They showed him Toby lying cold and alone in his grave, waiting for someone to find him, bring him home.

He stood up then, as if with motion he might outdistance this world's emptiness. He knew what it felt like to be left and he felt bad about leaving Lorie, but with the Blue Mood upon him he couldn't bear to endure *her* loneliness as well, disguised though it was as endless chatter. All the world's sorrow, it seemed, led back to Toby.

In case she needed another gin and tonic, he slipped three dollar bills under her glass, the rim of which bore the thin red stain of her lipstick.

He walked the length of the deck, taking the stairs down into the parking lot, skirting its edges until he found a path that curled between tall reeds, coming out upon a rubble-strewn dune and beyond that the rocky shoreline with its smell of death and decay.

Thinking maybe this was where the dream girl had fled, he followed the curve of the shore until he found himself behind the Beach and Tennis Club's bath house. From somewhere inside the fence came a low moaning sound, almost indistinguishable at first from the soft sighing of the wind but then clearly a separate sound, intermittent, repetitive, and unmistakably human.

Through a break in the wooden fence, he was able to reach the first of two tennis courts, the clay surface of which was badly pitted and uneven. The second of the courts was in even worse shape, the clay blackened and all but eroded, the net hanging in tatters.

On the wooden walkway between the men's and women's locker rooms, the doors to the shower stalls hung at jagged angles from their hinges or were missing altogether. Through the glass windows of the snack bar he saw counters littered with candy wrappers, eviscerated Dixie cups, a lone moldy French fry, empty soda bottles on their sides like fallen bowling pins.

At the pool he found the source of the moaning: a figure sprawled semi-upright against the ladder to the high diving board, arms draped loosely around the metal rungs, legs bent, the body sagging under its own weight.

When he reached the far end of the pool, past an obstacle course of lounge chairs pushed this way and that, he saw that it was Blevsky. The guy was in the slow-motion process of reaching above his head for the next rung. "Help me," he mumbled. "Help me."

"Help you do *what*?"

"Help me. . .get there."

"Where, Blevsky? Where the hell you think you're going?"

"Up." He raised his hand which wobbled in the air before pointing skyward. "Gonna take the plunge. Gonna do it."

"You *do* know there's no water in the pool, don't you? You'll kill yourself."

"S'okay. Nothin' to live for anyway." He lifted his head and grinned stupidly, the grin that had gotten him beaten up at least twice a week since first grade. He waggled his finger at the pool. "Water, see?"

What lay at the bottom of the pool, in addition to a half dozen deck chairs, a few orange life jackets, a pool skimmer and vacuum and assorted floats and rubber tubes, was about a foot of leaf-choked rain water, brownish-green in color.

"Gonna join the debris. It's debris for me."

For me, too, Hunt thought, weakening, giving in against his will to the Blue Mood. Someone help *me*. But who would that be?

"Come on, Blev." Hunt tried to pry him from the ladder but Blevsky gripped the rung and wouldn't let go. "You're drunk. Let's go home."

"I may be drunk but I've never been more loose—d."

"Lucid. The word is *lucid*."

"Thass what I said." He swayed against the ladder as if a wind were buffeting him.

"Let's go home."

"Can't. Can't go home."

"Why not?"

He had trouble getting the word out. "You—mill—ee—a—shun."

"What are you talking about?"

"One hun-red. In the parking lot, after I got thrown out. I hit one hun-red tonight. Who else you know got rejected one hun-red times?"

"No one."

"See?"

"No one because no one but you keeps score. It wouldn't hurt so much if you didn't keep score."

He stopped swaying to consider that. "You think so?"

"Besides, a hundred's a drop in the bucket. You know how many girls there are in the world? Millions. Hundreds of millions. You ever think of that? How many girls you haven't even asked yet?"

"No."

"Think about it." He wasn't sure what effect his words were having on Blevsky but he was making himself feel better. "You die, you won't have a chance to ask any of them out. And it'll be your fault, not theirs. You'll be the victim *and* the victimizer."

Hunt, still pulling at Blevsky to keep him from climbing, thought he felt the guy's hands loosening their grip. "Besides," he said, "success is ninety-nine percent failure. I read that somewhere."

"I don't get it."

"It only takes one to say yes. Only one."

He stared at Hunt, gaunt-eyed. "Then what?"

"You'll see. When it happens. You want to be around to find out, don't you?"

And then Blevsky let go of the ladder, trying to choke back his sobs, his full weight falling against Hunt.

—23—

The Castle Hill bus had just made a U-turn and sat idling beside McMann's parking lot where no more than a dozen cars now remained. Hunt moved slowly alongside the bus, Blevsky propped against him like a casualty of war.

When the driver saw Blevsky's condition he told Hunt, "You bring him on, he's your responsibility. He makes a mess, I don't open the doors till you clean it up. Understood?"

Hunt nodded, half-dragging, half-pushing his classmate up the steps. He deposited the fare, Blevsky hanging on him like a dead weight.

It was a struggle getting him down the aisle, Blevsky holding back and insisting for some reason they sit up front, Hunt thinking it wiser to be as far from the driver as possible lest he change his mind and throw them off. Finally he was able to push Blevsky into a seat by the back door, before taking a seat of his own across the aisle.

Through the window he could see across the parking lot to the deck, empty now, the fringes of the white umbrellas fluttering in the breeze. He closed his eyes, just to rest them and listened to the rattling sounds of the bus engine. His birthday had come and gone and here he was with not much to show for it, sometime before four in the morning, the sole occupant save one on the last bus home. There was some significance in that, he was sure, but for the moment he couldn't decide what it was.

When he opened his eyes he saw some movement on the deck. The door had opened and Lorie stood there, hesitating at first, looking left and then right, before crossing to the railing where, her back to him, reaching for the rail, she looked toward the lights of the bridge. He hoped she'd found Junie Moon, someone at least to withstand the torrent of words she was driven to release.

The doors wheezed closed and the bus eased onto the avenue.

When Hunt looked back, Lorie was still there: a small motionless figure gripping the rail, her blonde beehive tilting leftward in the wind.

Halfway down Castle Hill, with Blevsky snoring in the seat beside him, the Blue Mood returned once again. They were passing the construction site of the new housing development. Empty rubble-strewn lots surrounded the partially finished cluster of apartment buildings. Glass-less window sockets gaped from incomplete brick walls, the promise of anonymous uniformity in the process of being realized.

He had fallen between worlds again. Outside: the future's nightmare vision, and inside: this disembodied capsule of green and yellow light rushing him through the dark. It was the oddest kind of journey and he was being taken somewhere in ignorance, without his consent.

He fell into a game he played with himself, late like this when the night stretched long and wearisome: a solitary conversation in which he took both parts.

Q: What do we do?

A: We make a list. We wonder.

Q: What do we do tomorrow? And the day after?

108

A: We wait. We listen.

Q: For what?

Always, the conversation ended abruptly.

He was cold and afraid and immeasurably alone.

Maybe *this* was his tragic flaw. How low and sad he could get, how close it could bring him to inaction, to non-being.

He wrapped his arms tight across his chest to steady himself. He tried to shake himself free from the mood by remembering he was the Son of the King of Rock n' Roll and that someday he would return to this place, this ragged avenue, this changing borough.

And he would come bearing music and poetry. He would bring his 45s, kept clean and unscratched over the years, and his words that had been jammed into notebooks and scribbled on loose leaf, napkins, brown paper bags, whichever surface was available to him at the moments of inspiration.

And he would broadcast both, the music and the poems, to those who would remember the old days, as well as to those not yet born, and they would understand, the elders *and* the children—just as he would come to understand—what this journey was and where it was taking him.

PART THREE
SHAKE, RATTLE, AND ROLL

—24—

The first sign of trouble came when the bus drew near Chester Heights.

A row of choppers stood along the curb in front of the darkened Silver Goose Tavern. Milling around on the street and sidewalk were a dozen or more Golden Guineas. Through the bus window, Hunt watched as three black cars—a Caddy, a Chevy and a Dodge—pulled up and the gang members piled in. The small caravan, mufflers grumbling, ran the red light and made a sharp right into Chester Heights.

Hunt understood at least the rudiments of the situation. Whatever was going down would go down *inside* the housing development. The Golden Guineas were knowledgeable enough to know that bringing their bikes into Chester Heights would draw unwanted attention, especially from the development's foot patrol: a small cadre of unarmed security men whose fear first and foremost for their own well-being, and only secondarily for the safety of the residents, would prompt them to call in the NYPD from the nearby 43rd Precinct.

By the time the light changed and the bus chugged its way into Chester Heights, the three cars had vanished. At the Main

Oval, Hunt helped Blevsky off the bus. For the moment, at least, on the street around them, there was no sight of the Golden Guinea- mobiles.

Hunt, not wanting to press their luck, tried to hurry through the Oval. As always, he avoided the north end; but Toby returned nonetheless, insisting his presence be known.

He let go of Hunt's hand and, racing past benches and flower beds, he slipped under the chain onto the lawn. He knew he wasn't supposed to be there, knew playing on the Main Oval's grass wasn't allowed but he kept running in his bright shorts and T-shirt, giggling as he zig-zagged away from his big brother's outstretched hands, waiting for Hunt to grab him up in a soft tackle and bring him gently to the ground, the two of them rolling on the cool grass until one of the security men on foot patrol blew his sharp whistle and ended their fun.

Blevsky still needed help walking so their pace through the Oval was slow and made even slower by Blevsky's determination to get himself into the pool. It, too, was oval-shaped and rising from its center was a huge metallic fish in mid-leap, water spouting continuously from its open and over-sized mouth.

"Gotta go for a swim," he said. "S'hot. Gotta cool off. Gotta sober up. Gotta swim."

"You can't swim here," Hunt said, resorting again to reason and logic. "The water's only two feet deep."

"Don't care. Gotta cool off. Let me—"

They had reached the rim of the pool, the stillness broken by the steady slap and splash of water issuing from the mouth of the gigantic fish, running as it did down the shiny and slippery back, dripping into the water below. In recent years the pool had come to double as a wishing well, the bright blue bottom spotted with pennies, nickels, dimes and the occasional quarter.

Blevsky leaned over the rim like a dog straining on its leash, Hunt having all he could do to keep him from plunging in.

"The pool's closed," he said. "Look, there's nobody here,

right?" He pointed to the deserted park around them, hoping that silly rationale might deter the guy's efforts. "Tomorrow," he added. "Tomorrow you can go in," and temporarily at least that seemed to satisfy Blevsky's urge.

He stopped straining and let himself be drawn away from the rim. "Tomorrow," he said, as if it were a promise.

Hunt pushed him along the walkway and across the street. They passed Debby Ann's building and Hunt grimaced at the debacle of walking her home, feeling for the first time how long a night it had been.

Blevsky's building was the one behind hers. It would have been so much easier if the guy lived on the main floor but Hunt had to pull him into the elevator and prop him against the wall to keep him from collapsing, reaching out with his free hand to press the button for the sixth floor.

At 6F, Hunt went to push the apartment buzzer but Blevsky knocked away his hand. "Can't go in," he said.

"Why not?"

"Old man's there. Sees me like this, he'll kill me. Got to sober up first."

"Where?"

Blevsky looked at him dumbly. "Where what?"

"Where you going to sober up?"

"Here." He looked at the floor and began to lower himself on his wobbly pink legs, Hunt helping him down until he touched bottom.

Blevsky sat slumped against the dull green door, hands in his lap, eyes hazy and unfocused in the hall's pale light as Hunt backed away.

"Gotta sober up. Gotta swim."

Hunt stood at the end of the hall, waiting for the elevator. "Tomorrow."

"Time is it now?"

"Almost four."

"It *is* tomorrow." Blevsky tried to lift himself but fell back. "Help me. Old man'll kill me."

"Sleep it off," Hunt said, before disappearing into the elevator.

He was thinking about how to negotiate the few remaining blocks to his building without running into either the Golden Guineas or the Brandos. He didn't know which of the two he feared more.

—25—

Skirting the edge of the Oval, he saw the three black cars come cruising past on the avenue. He stopped in the shadow of the trees until they turned the corner, then he sprinted down the walkway and crossed the street.

Another walkway. This one between two sets of buildings.

A small oval.

A long alley.

When he arrived finally at his street, he saw Johnnie Jay sitting on the steps of his building.

"They're here," Johnnie Jay said.

"I know."

"You saw them?"

"By the Oval."

"You'll never guess who they're after."

"Who?"

"The Brandos in general. Your boy, Sal, in particular."

The news took Hunt by surprise. "How you know?"

"Ran into Flanagan again when I was parking the car. He got the scoop from a friend of his who's friends with Angelina Lanzalotto's brother."

"What do they have against Sal?"

"Plenty, from what I hear. Apparently two of the Golden Guineas are cousins of Angelina. They found out he was two-timing her with Debby."

Hunt gave a low whistle.

"Poetic justice, huh?" Johnnie Jay laughed. "Aristotle would have loved it. Man as the agent of his own destruction."

"Which makes his tragic flaw, what? His weenie?"

"Smallest one in the neighborhood, what I hear."

"Debby Ann doesn't seem to mind."

Johnnie Jay looked at him sharply. "Don't weaken."

"I'm working on it."

"Work harder." He stared Hunt down. "I mean, take a hard look, guy. She dumped all over you. She gave you *nothing*. She stood by and watched while you were about to get your ass kicked. You had *zilch* in common. You have to ask yourself what you were doing with her. It's like you were intentionally trying to beat yourself up, am I right?"

"But why—?"

"*You* tell me."

"If only she—"

"You've got this guilt thing, man. You like to punish yourself."

"Think so?"

"Here's my solution, buddy boy. Think of her at her worst. Like when she has rollers in her hair, or before she puts on her make-up. Think of a time when she looked really, really bad. Then tell me how cute she is."

Hunt was thinking about how she looked at McMann's. Dull-eyed and tired. Hair hanging flat and limp. Bangs a soggy mishmash on her forehead. A hint of a double chin already beginning to reveal itself. *That* was the future.

Bending from the waist, he gave Johnnie Jay an exaggerated bow. "Okay, your Highness. Your wish is my—whatever."

118

Johnnie Jay paused for dramatic effect, before delivering the juiciest of his news. "Word is, the Guineas are gonna do a number on Sal's testes."

"Jeez."

"I know, right?"

The thought of anyone messing with a guy's balls, even a mortal enemy's, made them both cringe.

"Come on," Johnnie Jay said. "Let's see what we can see."

From the roof they had a pigeon-eye view of the ball field below, a diamond at either end of its expansive oval shape. Originally a dirt field it had been recently tarred over, the black surface glinting where light from the street lamps reached. The tall chain-link fence that enclosed it was locked for the night, as were the playgrounds abutting the north and south sides of the field.

They could see across to the back wall of the power plant with its towering chimney spewing black smoke as it did every night in the wee small hours. In the morning a layer of soot would coat the field, thick enough to leave footprints.

There was no movement anywhere.

"So much for our intrepid security force," Johnnie Jay said.

"I wouldn't want to come up against the Golden Guineas with my bare hands, either. Would you?"

"That's not the point."

"What *is* the point?"

"The point is they're supposed to be on patrol, not hiding out in some hallway because they're too scared to show their faces. Hey, they want to run when the shit hits the fan, no problem. But they should be out here so they *know* what's going on. That way they could at least *call* the real cops."

For a few minutes there was a terrible stillness.

Hunt looked across the roofs of Chester Heights and beyond that to the lights of buildings farther west. The roof was where you came in search of possibility. He searched for it now in the miles and miles of hard brick thrust into a hazy, black sky.

Far below, the stillness was broken finally by a shout, the sound of footsteps.

Someone came running from an alley between buildings onto the walkway surrounding the ball field. He was followed quickly by seven or eight others, recognizable now as the Brandos, Sal the figure in the lead. They were being chased by four older guys with baseball bats, brawny hairy types in black denim and boots, bare-chested beneath their Golden Guinea-emblazoned leather vests.

It appeared the Brandos' strategy was to make a loop around the ball field, past the power plant and then make their escape by taking one of the walkways up to Tremont Ave and beyond. What they couldn't see, but what was obvious to Hunt and Johnnie Jay observing from above, was that they were running themselves into a trap.

At the south end of the ball field, the caravan of black cars with their lights out was moving slowly along the edge of the playground, past the row of handball courts and onto the walkway alongside the power plant, the three of them lining up to form a blockade hidden by the building's shadow.

They must have broken the lock on one of the parking lot gates because cars were forbidden on the walkways, so it would have come as a terrifying shock to Sal and the Brandos when six headlights flashed on out of the darkness, freezing them in the narrow stretch of no man's land between the two playgrounds: power plant on one side, ball field fence on the other.

Nowhere to run.

Golden Guineas coming behind them, Golden Guineas moving out of the shadows toward them.

As much as Hunt disliked Sal, he could feel his terror—the choked-off breathing, the icy grip on the heart: the down and out finality of knowing you were going to get it bad.

Sal tried to do an end run around them but someone tripped

him and he went down hard, besieged upon by a circle of guys bigger even than he was.

Meanwhile the other Brandos had been lined up along the ball field fence where a phalanx of Golden Guineas meted out a series of kicks, punches and jabs. Sal was yanked off the pavement and sent to join his fellows along the fence.

The next thing Hunt and Johnnie Jay saw was the row of Brandos dropping their pants. All of them, save Sal, turned to face the fence, bending forward, their fingers gripping the chain-links as a gauntlet of Golden Guineas hammered their bare, up-turned butts with Louisville Sluggers.

Sal's punishment came in the form of a frontal belt buckle assault.

Two of the Golden Guineas, presumably Angelina's cousins, took turns wielding their belts in such a way that the heavy metal buckle came in direct contact with the region of Sal's private parts. Instinctively Hunt pushed his hands down to defend his own vulnerable parts. Even from the roof, he could hear Sal's cries of pain, his body crumpling forward at every swing as he tried to use his meaty hands and arms for protection.

In a matter of minutes it was over.

The Golden Guineas got into their cars and drove off. Sal and the Brandos, underwear and jeans tangled around their ankles, were left slumped against the base of the ball field fence.

What Hunt would have preferred to think was that the beating might get Sal off his back, at least for a while. He knew, though, that was unlikely. If anything, this had only made things worse. Sal's humiliation here gave him *more* of a score to settle, when they finally met up.

He listened to the sobs and curses of the Brandos breaking the dark silence of that no man's land along the power plant wall.

121

At last the lamentations ceased.

When Hunt finally looked again over the roof wall, he saw the Brandos were gone. A lone security guard stood timidly on the ball field's far side, gazing at the spot where the assault had taken place. He nudged Johnnie Jay who made a snickering sound and said, "Our hero."

The sky above them had cleared. Here and there a few stars were visible. A late moon had risen. Hunt didn't feel ready to go home. He said, "I have to see it through."

Johnnie Jay, leaning with his back against the roof wall, squinted to read his intention. "See what through?"

"This night."

The wide open black sky seemed to be promising something. Exactly what that was, Hunt couldn't say. But something. Something was being promised. Or so he wanted to believe.

"I get it, man," Johnnie Jay said. "So what do you want to do?"

"I don't know. This was supposed to be the night for love."

Johnnie Jay offered his rueful smile. "Aren't they all?"

"But this was different. I had this—"

"Premonition? Inspiration? Hope?"

"Something like that."

"So what's it gonna be?"

"In a night of diminishing possibilities, the soul must continually re-invent itself."

Johnnie groaned. "A line from one of your poems?"

"One day. Maybe."

"So where does that leave us?"

"The Oval," Hunt said. "Let's take a stroll, the long way around past the school and the church, to clear our heads. Then hang out by the fountain a while." Even though—he was thinking—or maybe because, he knew Toby would be there.

And he was.

Picking a red flower from one of the beds. Holding it in his small fingers and offering it to Hunt.

"That's really pretty, Toby. That's really nice of you. But, you know, you're not supposed to pick the flowers. Because if everybody did that there wouldn't be any left for people to look at it and enjoy."

"More." Toby pointed to the long row of flowers on either side of the walkway.

"I know, Tobe. I know, but still—"

Toby ran on his short legs to the nearest bush and tried to pin the flower there.

"It's okay, Tobe. We can keep that one. It's okay this time."

Where the walkway turned, they found Augie asleep on one of the benches.

The kid opened his eyes before they got within twenty feet of him. "Who's sneakin' on me?"

Hunt didn't have to ask him what he was doing here, this late. It meant his parents had never come home. His eyes heavy with sleep, he was sitting up now, looking uncomfortable and staring at the ground, as if he'd been caught in a shameful act. "Can't a body get some rest without being harassed?"

"Just checking that you're all right," Hunt said.

Augie gave him his dead-eye, dead-pan look. "I'm peachy. Can't you tell?"

Before Hunt could ask if he wanted to go with them to the fountain, a commotion broke out in that direction.

Shouts.

The sound of water splashing.

More shouts.

Someone cursing.

All three of them stood on the bench for a better view. Beyond the flower beds and hedges, through a space in the trees, they could see the Brandos ranging ape-like along the rim of the pool, hurling things into the water. Between their hulking bodies, the object of their assault became visible.

Blevsky.

Crouched in the middle of the pool, he was using his raised hands and arms to deflect the barrage coming at him.

"We should split," Johnnie Jay said. "Before they see us."

Hunt watched the scene a moment longer before walking in the direction of the pool.

"Where you going?"

"Where do you think?"

"Don't be crazy, man, they'll kill you. They wanted to kill you *before* they got their asses kicked. You know how much they're going to want to kill you *now*?"

Dwelling on the details was something Hunt preferred not to do. "They'll have to catch me first."

Augie had run up alongside him. "I'm going, too."

"What for?"

He shrugged. "I want to."

"You awake enough to run?"

"You kidding me? I could outrun those dumb farts in a coma."

"It's only Blevsky," Johnnie Jay said, coming behind them. "He's used to taking this kind of abuse."

Hunt gave him a come-on-get-real look.

"Okay. Okay. So nobody deserves that kind of ridicule. Not even Blevsky."

From the walkway, they now had an unobstructed view of the scene. The Brandos had spread out to surround the pool, hooting and hollering, bombarding the still crouched Blevsky with refuse from the overflowing trash cans: beer bottles, soda cans, broken fragments from a hula hoop, a skate box, a hockey stick, whatever was large enough and solid enough to grip.

Blevsky, for his part, would rise intermittently and fling back at them whatever coins he could scrape from the pool's bottom. His Hawaiian shirt, drenched now, hung like a sack from his bony frame. Apparently the non-amphibious Brandos were waiting him out, hoping to drive him to shore where they could pounce on him with greater authority.

"So what's the plan?" Johnnie Jay wanted to know. "We stand up there. Let them use us as punching bags, or what?"

"Decoys," Hunt said. "You and Augie head to the north quadrant. I'll go to the south. Most likely they'll come after me. But if we split them up, that's good too."

"I'm going with *you*." Augie said it with the kind of determination Hunt knew there was scant hope arguing against.

"I don't want you getting hurt."

"I can outrun you—"

"I know, I know. In a coma, right?"

Augie stiffened. "I can take care of myself."

"I was kidding. Just kidding." To Johnnie Jay, Hunt said, "We'll meet up later on the church steps."

"What's left of us, yeah."

"Hey, we had one of the best track teams in the city, remember? You were the second best miler in St. Helena's history."

Johnnie Jay's sullen face remained unchanged by that reminder.

They followed the walkway toward the pool. When the trees fell away behind them, they stood in the open, in plain sight.

It was Sal, on the far side of the pool, who spotted them first. He uttered a loud, agonizing grunt, pointing with his left hand, the other Brandos turning to face them, Sal cocking his right arm, the beer bottle originally intended for Blevsky now the subject of a down field pass that easily cleared the water, splintering on the walkway, shards scrambling across the pavement to within several feet of the three decoys.

That set the flight plan in motion.

Across a bed of tulips, through a row of waist-high hedges, jumping benches and the low loops of chain that served as keep-off-the-grass fences, Hunt and Augie took off for the south end of the Oval.

Johnnie Jay fled in the opposite direction, drawing only two pursuers.

Which left seven of them in pursuit of Hunt and Augie.

—27—

What Hunt had been counting on, in addition to his and Augie's superior speed, was that the Brandos would be hampered by their injuries. And they were. They got off to a slow start, Sal the slowest of them all, hobbling as he ran, bringing up the rear.

What Hunt *hadn't* counted on was the extent of their need to compensate for their earlier humiliation which seemed to intensify as they gave chase. Instead of giving up as Hunt had hoped, they kept on coming like a slow lumbering herd of rhinos.

"The South tunnels," he told Augie as they left the Oval behind. His breath came in short, ragged gasps. "We can hide out there."

They reached the avenue, running full speed, the Brandos some three or four hundred feet behind. A long flight of stairs led down into the south oval, a wide expanse of fenced-off grass surrounded by trees and benches, deserted now as were all the streets and walkways.

The building they were heading for was on the lawn's far side. He glanced at the boy keeping pace beside him. The kid

127

was true to his word: he could run. He kept his head down, his arms and legs pumping hard, and there was no sign he was tiring.

In the game of predator and prey, Hunt had learned, it was always a matter of gambling. It wasn't only skill that saved you. It was luck. Which meant that, of necessity, there would be times your luck ran out. He hoped this wouldn't be one of those times.

They entered the building, going directly down into the basement which was a series of interconnecting storage rooms that held bikes, sleds, baby carriages, wagons and other over-sized children's toys.

The tunnels were on the level below.

They were a collection of hallways that had been built as a fall-out shelter in case of nuclear attack. You could travel underground all the way across Chester Heights, *if* you could get down in there. The facilities department kept the doors locked but they were always going down to do routine maintenance and often forgot to lock them. This was a gamble Hunt was taking, finding a door unlocked, because the tunnels were the ultimate solution for a clean getaway. They would be able to surface nearly a mile away, without ever having set foot on the street.

His back-up plan was that if the doors were locked they would simply hide in one of the storage rooms.

So they moved now through the first of the dimly lit rooms, Hunt using his shoe to break the occasional light bulbs that hung from the ceiling pipes, leaving behind them a trail of darkness.

They had made it partway through the second storage room when they heard noises behind them, muffled at first but soon taking the form of exclamatory curses and then footsteps.

Hunt put his finger to his lips and they moved faster, treading lightly.

There were four such rooms before they reached a door down into the tunnels.

One of the Brandos shouted from the darkness behind them, "I hear them. I hear the sons-a-bitches."

This last of the carriage rooms had been emptied—the four bare walls in the process of being re-painted, a ladder and paint cans stacked against one wall. No place to hide here, if it came to that.

The door to the tunnels stood against the far wall and in moving toward it they passed over a grate, below which a section of tunnel was visible. Safety within sight, if only they could get there.

The door handle wouldn't turn. *Locked.*

Hunt had run them into a trap.

They were cornered.

And there was nowhere in this barren room to hide.

In the next moment, though, Augie slipped around him, sliding a key into the lock and opening the door.

Hunt was dumbfounded but said nothing until they closed the door behind them and took the metal stairs down into the fall-out shelter.

The lighting was dim, a single naked bulb protruding from the wall every thirty or forty feet, the tunnel itself a barren chasm: alternating patches of darkness and light as far as the eye could see.

They sat on the foot of the stairs to catch their breath. Hunt was thinking about Johnnie Jay, hoping that he too had made it to safety. The guy could outrun almost anyone, despite his crooked walk.

Now Hunt turned to Augie who sat on the step below. "So where'd you get a key?"

Augie shrugged. The key had already disappeared back inside his pocket.

"I never heard about anyone having a key. Except the maintenance men."

"Yeah," was all Augie would say.

"You steal it or what?"

"Got my ways."

Hunt stared at him: the small face, the dark eyes, the flat nose, his lips like a lock on his mouth. "You amaze me some-times, you know that?"

"Amaze myself sometimes."

"You saved our ass."

"Yeah."

Hunt envied the kid his composure. "No big deal, right?"

"When you the only black kid in a white neighborhood, you always saving your ass. Nobody else gonna do it."

Footsteps sounded above them and Hunt raised his hand for silence. Boots made a clinking sound on the grate. The door handle was jiggled. The flat of a hand struck the door, then something heavier, a shoulder. Boots kicked low and furiously against the metal.

"He beat us again," one of the Brandos said in disgust.

"The more he wins, the more he loses," Sal said. "He owes us. Big time now."

There was the sound of a beer can being opened.

"Hey, gimme some of that," someone—Hunt thought it sounded like Rudy—said.

"Me first," Sal said.

A silence followed.

The smacking of lips.

"We got that other thing to do now," Sal said.

"The bums, you mean?"

"Stinkin' up the neighborhood."

Another voice said, "How many times we got to bust them up before they get the message?"

And another, "They got one more, I hear. A Rican. What's that make? Five?"

"Five too many," Sal said. "Like rats. They take over."

Someone thumped across the floor. Someone coughed.

"Come on," Sal said.

The rustle of creaking leather.

Bodies in motion.

Boots crossed the grate.

Footsteps faded into silence.

In the dim underground light, Augie said, "What now?"

Hunt was already in motion, moving down the long hall through the checkered light of the netherworld. Augie ran to catch up.

"*You're* going home to get some sleep. Kids your age aren't supposed to be up all hours of the night."

"No way. I'm going, too. They're kin to me."

"Who?"

"The homeless guys."

"How you figure that?"

"Nobody wants *them* here, either."

—29—

The Tattered Ones were asleep along the station wall, their makeshift mattresses in line like cots in a dormitory.

Alphonso had the most luxurious of the accommodations—a set of old sofa cushions for a mattress, a rolled-up bath towel for a pillow, a shower curtain as bed cover—and it was he who Hunt awakened first.

He did so gently: a tap on the shoulder, a whispered "*Alphonso.*" He didn't want the man to think it was a raid.

The old poet stirred uneasily, then bolted upright, his back pressed hard to the wall, his eyes blinking fearfully. In the motion, his homburg slipped from his head. He'd once told Hunt the first rule of homeless living was that you slept with your most prized possessions on your body, the harder for thieves to get at them.

"You have to leave," Hunt told him. "It's not safe."

"Who? Them greasers?"

"The Brandos, yes."

"They got nothing better to do?" His breath was thick, wine-soured. "Shoulda told their mothers on them."

"Hurry," Hunt said.

Augie had wakened the others who were in various stages of coming to.

"*Donde?*" the last in line, a vacant-eyed man, asked.

Hunt had never seen him before. The newest member, he assumed. The Puerto Rican man the Brandos had mentioned. "Upstairs. We've got to hurry."

The men moved slowly, grumbling to themselves, fumbling through their belongings once they got to their feet. Only Jumbo, the thinnest and frailest of them, was still on the ground.

With Hunt on one side, Augie on the other, they brought the man to his feet where he stood dazed and wobbling, from sickness or intoxication it was hard to tell. "Help him up the stairs," Hunt said.

"I gotta go," Mr. Pee said.

"No time now." Hunt moved among them in the dim under-shadows of the station, urging them toward the stairs.

They had formed a ragged line, Alphonso leading the way, Augie bringing up the rear with Jumbo. Hunt ran up the steps ahead of them to the token booth on the middle landing. The attendant was asleep, grousing at Hunt for waking him, taking his annoyed, sweet time sliding the tokens through the window slot.

Hunt deposited the tokens as the men passed through the turnstile, then ushered them up the next flight of stairs to the platform, deserted at this time of a Saturday morning. Far down the track he thought he saw the light of a down-bound train moving toward them. Overnight schedules were spotty; you could easily wait a half hour between trains. They needed some luck.

From the platform he had a panoramic view of the dark, hulking buildings of Chester Heights, all one hundred and seventy-one of them, a fortress against night's solitude. On the street below the Brandos arrived, some by car, the rest on foot. Like a pack of rabid dogs, they converged on the circular plaza below the station. It would be only a matter of moments before they figured out where the homeless men had fled.

134

The light on the tracks had grown larger, brighter. A train was indeed on its way.

On the platform, the Tattered Ones had formed a loose semi-circle around Hunt. Several of them carried possessions: Alphonso, for one, clutching his battered notebook; O'Shea carrying some kind of stuffed animal; the new man, Luis, appearing to be holding something in his clenched fist.

"Gotta go," Mr. Pee said and started to wander off down the platform in search of a modicum of privacy.

From below came the shouts and curses of the Brandos as they ransacked the encampment.

"Not now, Mr. Pee," Hunt called after him. "You have to wait."

The Manhattan-bound train was approaching the station. It was an express—another stroke of luck. No way their assailants could catch them with the local that would follow this one.

Hunt ran after Mr. Pee to bring him back.

It was only after he and Augie had gotten them safely inside the train that Hunt could breathe a sigh of relief.

Through the window, as the train left the station, he saw the first of the Brandos reach the top of the stairs and step out onto the platform.

—30—

The five homeless men sat on one side of the aisle, Hunt and Augie on the other. A heavy, sullen silence had fallen upon them, a post-climactic lethargy enhanced by the car's febrile yellow light and the blackness of the tunnel through which they were traveling.

They had moved to the first car where there were no other passengers. Hunt thought they were less likely to be bothered there, and it was safer too, this close to the conductor.

Fearing the onset of another Blue Mood, he forced himself up and stood at the front window, the long tunnel unfolding before him, blackness everywhere save for intermittent pinpricks of light, red or yellow or green, that seemed to vanish almost as soon as they appeared. He knew there was symbolism in that and that one day he might write about it; but at the moment his mind was a disembodied and unblinking eye, in observation mode only, forsaking interpretation. This was the night for love, or so it had been deemed; there would be time for reflection later.

It was Alphonso who supplied the poetry this night.

Hunt had returned to his seat and was staring across the

aisle at him as the old man, in turn, stared back at him. Perhaps his alcohol-infused torpor had lifted enough for him to see himself and his fellow Tattered Ones in all of their grim hopelessness, tight-lipped and bleary-eyed, slouched as they were in various positions of humbled introversion: O'Shea clutching his stuffed animal like a baby, Luis with his clenched fists, Jumbo frail and shriveled and turned inward as if he might evaporate there on his seat right before their eyes, and Mr. Pee pressing his palms between his legs. They were homeless twice over now. Homeless within the state of homelessness.

So in the face of despair where does a literary man turn? To his scribblings, of course, and Alphonso began thumbing through his notebook in search of the appropriate words to characterize their condition.

Mr. Pee could wait no longer. Apologizing profusely to anyone who might be listening, he shuffled down the aisle to the only lavatory available: the open space between cars. When he returned he sat down and closed his eyes, a nirvana-like peace settling over his face, the kind of peace only a man with an enlarged prostate can comprehend.

By this time Alphonso was already on his feet, brow furrowed in concentration, notebook tucked under his arm, having failed to find there the appropriate verse for the occasion. With staggering steps calibrated to the train's rocking motion, moving slowly up and down the aisle, making eye contact with no one, he extemporized:

> *My home whines like a hurt cat,*
> *Rattles like a nasty wind,*
> *Spinning through depths of darkness*
> *Who could have foreseen,*
> *These tunnels taking us to our eternal unrest*
> *Where morning offers no comfort*
> *Where daylight is but another form of motion*
> *And life is but this elegy on wheels*

The men, each in his own way, remained stone-faced and

non-committal, turned inward except for Luis whose blank stare focused on the flickering blackness beyond the windows.

Even in the most abysmal moment of their youth, who of them could have foreseen this, Hunt wondered, that one June day of an impossible future they would be riding the subway at five in the morning, without benefit of wife or family or four walls to keep them safe? *Who?*

And what would they do now without even a subway station wall to lie down beside?

Augie had been scrutinizing the men, as well. His nose was pinched against the unsanitary smell coming from across the aisle. He seemed to have reached some kind of conclusion about each of them, but it was the round-faced, chubby-cheeked O'Shea that he addressed. "What *is* that thing?"

At first the man seemed confused, so accustomed was he to the companionship of his inanimate friend. "Oh, Wilhelmina, you mean. She's a Wallaby."

"A walla *who*?"

"A Wallaby. Basically a smaller version of a kangaroo. A mammal of the marsupial order. Pouch-bearing." He held the brownish-grey imitation propped on his knee so that it was facing Augie. With his thumb, he pried open the pouch on its chest. "Her teats are hidden in here. This is where she nurses her young. They're completely protected."

Augie made a face. "What are they, faggots or something? They can't look out for their own selves?"

"It's nature's way of preserving the species."

Augie turned away in disgust. "Screw nature."

Hunt leaned close to him, whispered, "Be nice. They're your kin, remember?"

"In Australia, we have all manner of interesting and unusual animals," O'Shea was saying.

"Yeah, yeah, I know," Augie said. "Kangaroos and Koala bears."

O'Shea's eyes ignited, his cheeks flushed. "Oh, many more than that. Those are simply the most well-known. For example, we have other note-worthy marsupials such as wombats, Tasmanian devils and numbats. We even have a *black* Swan. Have you ever seen a black swan? Nature's mistake, some people call it. Disarmingly exotic and chillingly mysterious. A contradiction in terms, you might say. It gives one pause."

He drifted into thought, his eyes shining, before rushing on. "We have wild dogs called Dingoes and something called the Blob Fish which many believe is the ugliest animal on the planet. And there's your exceedingly rare Blue-tongued lizard, and your Tawny Frog-mouth, a bird of prey like an owl but in the forest you can't tell it from a dead tree stump. And there's your Kookaburra bird whose call sounds exactly like human laughter. It's also known as the laughing jackass." He settled back in the seat triumphantly. "Oh, we have animals you can't imagine."

For once, Hunt thought, Augie seemed chastened. No wise-ass remark at the ready. If anything, he sat reverently still as if he might be contemplating the array of oddities O'Shea had presented. After a moment he reached into his back pocket for his dictionary and began looking up words.

Everyone else remained silent, as well. At the 149th Street station and at 125th several people came into the car, but seeing the motley assortment before them, turned back and chose another one. At this point Augie had put away the dictionary, his face as somber and as inward-directed as the older men across the aisle.

What followed was the long non-stop stretch to 59th during which the train picked up speed, rocking on its rails, local stations flicking by in a dull poisonous light, an occasional isolated face illuminated for an instant before being lost beyond the windows. The silence among them grew even heavier and more morose than before. Hunt imagined a collective Blue Mood must have overtaken them all.

It was Jumbo who broke the silence, taking out his harmonica and playing some notes, something deep and slow and blue, before interrupting himself to say: "This 'bout a man named

Dupree. Had a girl named Betty and she done beg him and beg him for a diamond ring. Dupree, he loves her powerful bad but gots no money so he takes his .45, goes to the jewelry store and shoots a man. Gives the ring to Betty and tries to leave town but they catches him, puts him in the jail. Tells the judge it was the jelly roll done him in. Judge nods and say he understand, he understand very well, but has him hanged anyways. Betty done cry and cry and cry, and finds herself another man. . . .They say Dupree done died from the heartbreakin' blues."

Jumbo raised the harmonica to play again, a sound both mournful and defiant, rising to fill the empty spaces of the car, insisting itself against the rollicking click of the rails, the harsh and brutal whine of brakes on metal, the terrible silence that had befallen them. It seemed to Hunt as if a question had been raised and it hung in the air unanswered until Augie added the sound of his harmonica, tentative at first, following Jumbo's lead, but growing stronger and more assured as he caught on.

Then, as abruptly as the tune had begun, it ended. Jumbo sank back in the seat as if he'd exhausted himself, the hand holding his instrument falling to his lap, his face seeming to cave in, his eyes half-closed. His breath came slow and heavy. "It all begin and end in the Delta," he said.

"What does?" Hunt asked but the man didn't answer.

Within moments, the men had returned to their own worlds. The melancholy of Betty and Dupree's tale was re-incarnated in the train's persistent clamor, as was the uncertainty of their own survival on the streets. Or so it was in Hunt's rumination. What would happen to them tomorrow? And the day after?

Later, Hunt would think that the returning silence must have been too unbearable for Augie, because without notice the kid began playing again. Nothing downbeat or plaintive this time. Nothing like Jumbo's blues.

What came bursting from between his lips was up-tempo, a series of percussive blasts with a catchy beat.

Bop bop ba
Bop bop ba

bop bop ba-ba-ba
Bop bop ba-ba-ba
Bop bop ba
Bop bop ba

The sound stirred the blood of the aging men, Jumbo the first to be revived, breathing into his harmonica once more, this time following Augie's lead, having to dial up the beat to keep up with the kid.

Mr. Pee shuffled off to relieve himself again and when he returned the music had grown even more raucous and insistent: Hunt nodding his head to keep time, Alphonso scribbling furiously in his notebook, O'Shea holding Wilhelmina like a puppet on his lap, manipulating her front paws in time with the percussive blasts of the harmonica. Only Luis remained immune, listening—in that region far behind his eyes—to a music of his own.

Mr. Pee took hold of the pole as if it were a dance partner and swung himself halfway around it, spilling forth a vocal track of his own invention.

"Roll, rattle and rock
Rock, rattle and roll
What we gotta do
to save our doggone souls?"

At the City Hall station, they parted ways. "You guys should be all right for now," Hunt told them. "Ride this all the way out to Flatbush. By the time you turn around and get back to 177th it'll be daylight. The Brandos will be gone."

"What about tomorrow night?" Alphonso asked.

Tomorrow and tomorrow and tomorrow. Hunt wished he knew. "We'll have to figure out something, won't we?" he said.

"Come with us," Alphonso said. "Come with us out to Brooklyn."

"Told Johnnie Jay I'd meet him at the church," Hunt said.

"Don't want him to worry. Besides," he nodded at Augie who returned his concern with a grimace, "this kid's got to get some sleep."

He waved to them through the window as the express pulled out. None of the men seemed to notice.

O'Shea stared at the wallaby in his arms.

Jumbo stared at the harmonica in his hands.

Alphonso stared at a page of his notebook.

Vacant-eyed Luis stared at the floor.

—31—

The first two Brandos came for Hunt from the far end of the platform.

In the dull pre-dawn light they stepped away from the 177th Street sign and approached at an unhurried pace, grinning.

Hunt froze: heartbeat skittering, what felt like a chasm breaking open in his gut. Augie had stopped several feet behind him.

For the merest fraction of a second, the world was at a standstill. On the subway ride, exhaustion had overtaken him but now Hunt's fast-beating heart propelled him into motion. One more flight from the enemy. One more escape.

The doors of the express that had carried them back had already closed. The train began to gather speed as it moved away from the station.

So side by side, Hunt and Augie ran for the stairs.

Halfway down, Augie jumped to the landing below. Hunt scuttle-jumped three or four steps at a time, one hand sliding on the banister. At the mid-level landing they opted for jumping the turnstiles rather than use the rotating circular gateway, too slow an exit.

"Hey!" a voice called from the token booth but they had already reached the final set of stairs where they drew up sharply.

Staring at them from ground level were Sal and four of the Brandos.

Cautiously, Hunt began to back-pedal.

First to bolt was Augie, Hunt right behind him. They came running back across the landing, jumping the turnstiles a second time. "Hey!" the voice yelled from the token booth. "Hey, yous!"

The two Brandos from the platform were waiting on the uptown stairs, so their only option was the downtown side.

It was clear to Hunt that now the only way out was to use the tracks. When they reached the platform, they split up: Hunt running to the north end, Augie to the south. The idea was to take the small set of steps that led down onto the tracks, then use the narrow edge that ran alongside the railing. You had to time it right. You had to get to the next station before a train came through or else it was curtains. But they were both fast and they had done it before. They knew beyond doubt they could outrun the Brandos, *if*—and this was highly doubtful in the Brandos' present condition—they tried to pursue.

That was the plan.

Hunt, halfway down the platform, heard Augie cry out behind him.

Shouts, trampling feet.

When he turned he saw Augie pulling himself up from the platform floor. He began limping forward but within moments the Brandos were on him.

Hunt stopped running.

He stood there watching Sal and one of his buddies pulling a squirming Augie toward him, the rest of the Brandos lining up behind them.

"You or the kid," Sal shouted down the platform. "What's it gonna be?"

There was, Hunt knew, no guarantee they would spare the boy even if he surrendered, so he said, "First, let the kid go."

144

"No way."

"Sign of good faith," Hunt said. "At least take your hands off him."

"No way, loser. Not till I whip your ass."

Hunt considered his options.

The game of predator and prey. This time his gamble hadn't paid off. He'd simply run out of luck.

The beating began on the empty platform. If it had been a weekday, there would have been someone around to call the police, but this early on a weekend morning Hunt was on his own.

They came at him from all sides; it was like fighting back against a merry-go-round. He swung wildly at the carousel of fury that whirled around him. Fists and arms and knees and boots, a non-stop barrage. The air went out of him more times than he could count.

He gasped for breath. He thought he might vomit.

His head was ringing, the aftermath—or so it seemed—of someone taking a hammer to it, the contents of his skull turned upside down, feeling loose and broken and scattered. He couldn't tell which part of him hurt more or where he was more afraid of being hit.

At one point he staggered free of them, making his way to the head of the stairs, where they caught up with him again, Sal taking over, each blow it seemed carrying the full weight of his thick upper body, Hunt grasping for the banister to keep himself upright, Sal hammer-chopping him, driving him down step by step, Hunt aware of a crushing weight applied again and again to his neck and shoulders.

His legs buckled under him, no longer able to support his body. His vision dimmed and blurred and dimmed again, his consciousness ebbing away in receding waves, until he finally struck something hard, unyielding.

He thought it might cease now, the falling, the pounding in

his head, his ears, the nausea like a bottomless chasm opening and re-opening in his gut.

It didn't.

Not yet.

Not then.

His face was pressed against the floor, the grit and grime of it finding a way inside his mouth, under his tongue. Something was jabbing at his ribs, his legs. Something came down flat and hard on his back.

Then he couldn't move.

There was a moment when he couldn't see, when the aching soreness and hurt in his bones pushed him beyond thought of any kind, beyond awareness of anything but his pain.

From the other side of that pain—from far, far away—someone was calling to him. The voice was faint but insistent. It took a moment to realize it was Toby. *With his wide crooked grin, reaching his arms toward him, offering words of comfort.*

Then something soft touched his head, something had hold of his arm.

Through the dim haze of his vision he saw now that it was Augie. Trying to help him. Trying to get him on his feet.

PART FOUR
EARTH ANGEL

—32—

The police came finally—a squad car with two officers—having been called by the man in the token booth. They found Hunt sitting on the subway steps, his head resting in his hands, Augie sitting beside him.

They asked him if he knew his assailants. *Yes, he did.*

Did he want to press charges? *No, he didn't.*

And why was that? *It was a personal thing.*

Was he sure about that? *Yes, he was.*

Did he want to go to the hospital? *No, he didn't.*

Was he sure about that? *Yes, he was.*

Did he want them to call his parents, have someone come get him? *That wouldn't be necessary.*

Hunt finally raised his head, blinked in the shadowy light of the steps to clear his vision which had improved somewhat, save for some wavering at the margins. He wished he could blink away the head pain as easily. "I have somewhere I have to be," he said.

The older of the two officers leaned toward him. He had dark, bushy eyebrows with flecks of grey, and strong dark eyes. "You mean an appointment or something?"

"An appointment, yes. Sort of."

The officer looked at Augie with suspicion. "This kid with you?"

"Yes."

"You should see a doctor, fellah. You really should."

"Later. Maybe later."

The officer gave Hunt an I-don't-understand-you-kids-now-adays look. "You want a ride to this. . .*appointment* of yours?"

"I can walk, thanks."

"Okay, okay." He gave a sigh of resignation, taking off his hat and running his fingers through his thick, greying hair. He let his eyes roam over the ravaged collection of cardboard, newspapers and cushions where the homeless men had slept. "What a pigsty."

"Everyone needs a bed," Hunt said.

"Yeah, yeah, yeah." The officer put on his hat and stepped back. "Stay out of trouble, kid, you hear?"

"Do my best," Hunt said.

—33—

His feet were the only part of his body without aches or pains but that didn't mean he could walk in a straight line. Every other bone and muscle cried out in protest when he moved so that his efforts were more of a shuffle than a walk, at times a kind of halting sporadic side-step, a delicate balancing act with the aim of maximizing comfort, minimizing hurt. On occasion he had to stop and rest his hand on Augie's shoulder to steady himself.

Around them, Chester Heights was in the process of a slow, early morning awakening. Lights had begun to appear in the casement windows. On the street older men stood in line at the stationery store for the morning paper. From the corner bakery the warm, sweet smells of brown sugar and cinnamon drifted out from the racks of oven-fresh hot cross buns, crumb cakes and crullers.

"You hungry?" he asked Augie.

"No."

"Me, neither."

He was thinking—in the foggy way he was able to think in his present condition—that turning eighteen had proven to be

151

far different than he thought it would be, that among the things the night had taught him was this: being a man wasn't a matter of having a girl to love, so much as it was not letting your own sorrow keep you from doing what needed to be done.

And that made him think of the Tattered Ones and how they might survive future attacks from the Brandos. No doubt they would have to vacate the station at night. There would be no one, certainly not the police, to protect them. He thought they might find sanctuary in the vacant lots along Castle Hill Ave, or maybe on the shoreline behind the Beach and Tennis Club. Or maybe even the abandoned club itself—at least until the developers came in. That way they would still be in the neighborhood, tucked away safely at night, yet close enough to rattle their cups under the station during business hours. He would be sure to suggest that to Alphonso.

As for himself, he thought perhaps the Brandos would leave him alone now. They'd done their number on him. They'd made their point. And Sal would be leaving in a month for football training camp at Villanova. Besides, what motivation for vengeance did he have now that Hunt was no longer pursuing Debby Ann? Hunt had begun to think of her as an error in judgment. He liked that phrase, *error in judgment*, because of its suggestion of choice. You may have committed such an error once, but there was no reason to believe you would make the same error a second time.

Beyond the row of buildings ahead, the brick wall of the church had become visible. He was able to walk a little bit easier now. It wasn't that the pain had lessened—he didn't think it had—but he was getting used to it. He was learning how to accommodate it.

Soon in the early morning light he had a clear view of the church steps. He blinked his eyes to be sure.

No sign of Johnnie Jay.

152

—34—

From the steps of the church, in what was left of his battered tux, Hunt watched the sun lift above the roofs of Chester Heights, dripping a silver-gold light down the long walls of brick, too bright for him to look at. His body still cried out with pain and soreness, but what he was thinking was that his parents were going to kill him not only for staying out so late and for coming home in this condition, but also because he'd spent nearly two-thirds of his paycheck.

Johnnie Jay was still nowhere in sight.

Except for Augie sitting beside him, his only company were the parishioners arriving early for morning mass, glancing at him with abbreviated curiosity as they rushed up the steps into the vestibule.

Augie, silent and withdrawn as usual, held his hands between his knees, running his fingers absently over his harmonica. He stared out toward the street and the elevated tracks beyond. For the first time since being awakened on the bench, the kid looked beat, the long hours of night finally catching up with him.

"Don't you think you should go home?"

Augie looked at him without blinking. "What for?"

"You need some sleep. Your folks will be worried." Hunt kept looking at him, at the hard stare which, if anything, had grown harder over the course of the night. "You really need to get some rest."

"Look better than you do."

Hunt could imagine. "I don't look too hot, do I?"

"No."

"Imagine how I'd look if Sal hadn't gotten his balls hammered."

"You might be dead."

"Guess I'm lucky, after all."

"You got the same luck as me," Augie said without expression.

Hunt laughed then. "You never say thank you to anybody, do you?"

"For what?"

Hunt laughed again. "It's okay. I didn't do it only for you."

"For who then?"

"Someone I knew." He corrected himself, remembering Toby's sudden appearance on the subway steps, remembering what Johnnie Jay had said in the cemetery: it's not something you have to run away from. *At the bottom of the church steps now, Toby stood without judgment of any kind, his arms spread wide, waiting to be lifted up, waiting to be held.* "Someone I know."

Then, looking up, he saw the Vision, the dream girl, coming up the steps toward him. She had changed into a white blouse and a pleated skirt that reached below her knees. When she saw his face she put her hand to her mouth, said: "O God, you're hurt."

She began rummaging through her purse and pulled out a small package of tissues. "Wait," she said before hurrying up the stairs.

In a moment she was back, kneeling beside him, cupping his chin with one hand, as she dabbed at his forehead with a

154

moistened tissue. "Thank God for holy water," she said. "What happened to you?"

"Life happened."

"You should see a doctor. You really should."

His face felt sore all over. Her touching it even lightly made him grimace and pull back but the cool moisture on his skin was comforting. Then Augie was helping too, bringing holy water down the steps in his cupped hands, as she used the tissues to clean the dirt from his cuts.

"What kind of fight were you in?" she asked.

"The losing kind."

"It's not funny," she said.

But it was, he thought, it was kind of funny in a way. "I saw you earlier," he said.

"At the dance, you mean?"

"At the Rat, too. At McMann's. You were always flitting by, and vanishing."

"Probably looking for my sister. She's always running off somewhere."

She dabbed around his eyes and he closed them a moment against the pressure. "How come I've never seen you before? Before tonight, I mean?"

"We just moved here."

"Welcome to the neighborhood," he said with a laugh.

"There's a lot to adjust to." Her brow tightened in concentration. "I tell myself I'm still the same person. Moving to a new place doesn't change that. At least that's what I've read. Who you are *always* catches up to you. That's what all the best books say."

He studied her face, how serious it got when she was making a point. "You read a lot, huh?"

"I do." She blushed. "All kinds of things."

Up close like this, her face inches from his, she was no vision at all, simply a beautiful girl with clear, dark eyes and when she smiled at him it was a wide and hopeful smile, without qualification.

"I didn't know if you were real."

She looked at him as if she didn't understand. "I'm real, all right. My name's Vera."

From the street Johnnie Jay was yelling to him. "I went looking for you. When you didn't show, I went looking. Those assholes never got near me." When he reached the curb, he stopped short at the sight of Hunt's face, at the sight of Vera kneeling beside him. "Oh God—"

The church bells were ringing.

She put her tissues back in her purse. "Please see a doctor. I mean it. I really do."

Hunt wanted to tell her about Toby, and the Blue Mood, about how birthdays—even one so important as your eighteenth—come and go, just another day when nobody knows how fast your heart is beating. But he would save that for another time.

She stood above him and watched him with eyes softened by concern.

"I'll call you, Vera. I'll call you soon," he said before she turned to run lightly up the steps to the seven o'clock mass.

Philip Cioffari is the author of the novels: THE BRONX KILL; DARK ROAD, DEAD END; CATHOLIC BOYS; JESUSVILLE; and the short story collection, A HISTORY OF THINGS LOST OR BROKEN, which won the Tartt First Fiction Prize, and the D. H. Lawrence award for fiction. His short stories have been published widely in commercial and literary magazines and anthologies, including *North American Review, Playboy, Michigan Quarterly Review, Northwest Review, Florida Fiction*, and *Southern Humanities Review*. He has written and directed for Off and Off-Off Broadway. His Indie feature film, which he wrote and directed, LOVE IN THE AGE OF DION, has won numerous awards, including Best Feature Film at the Long Island Int'l Film Expo, and Best Director at the NY Independent Film & Video Festival. He is a Professor of English, and director of the Performing and Literary Arts Honors Program, at William Paterson University. www. philipcioffari.com

www.ingramcontent.com/pod-product-compliance
Lightning Source LLC
Chambersburg PA
CBHW031202260626
47169CB00004B/1213